DETROIT PUBLIC LIBRARY

3 5674 00686256 0

W9-CAD-906

DETROIT PUBLIC LIBRARY

BL

DATE DUE

THE ALDEBURG CÉZANNE

TH

ALDEBURG CÉZANNE

JOHN ALEXANDER GRAHAM

An *Atlantic Monthly Press* Book

Little, Brown and Company — Boston — Toronto

C1

S

COPYRIGHT © 1970 BY JOHN ALEXANDER GRAHAM

ALL RIGHTS RESERVED. NO PART OF THIS BOOK MAY BE REPRODUCED
IN ANY FORM OR BY ANY ELECTRONIC OR MECHANICAL MEANS INCLUD-
ING INFORMATION STORAGE AND RETRIEVAL SYSTEMS WITHOUT PERMIS-
SION IN WRITING FROM THE PUBLISHER, EXCEPT BY A REVIEWER WHO
MAY QUOTE BRIEF PASSAGES IN A REVIEW.

ATLANTIC—LITTLE, BROWN BOOKS
ARE PUBLISHED BY
LITTLE, BROWN AND COMPANY
IN ASSOCIATION WITH
THE ATLANTIC MONTHLY PRESS

*Published simultaneously in Canada
by Little, Brown & Company (Canada) Limited*

PRINTED IN THE UNITED STATES OF AMERICA

MAR 15 '71

BL

For my parents

Only the settings in this book are real. I've tried to describe accurately the geography of the Metropolitan Museum and its surroundings, but there the attempt at verisimilitude has ended. The characters are products of my own imagination, and I've intended no resemblance whatsoever to any of the employees of that great museum.

THE ALDEBURG CÉZANNE

ONE

"You're looking at it, scout," the guard said, demonstrating vast intimacy with the walls and doors.

"That's *it*?" Roger Murray said, pointing to the door he'd been unsuccessfully trying to locate for the last twenty minutes. "Why don't they put up a sign? 'European Paintings Department' or something. There isn't a mark on it. It could be a broom closet."

"That's so you won't get any uninvited guests." The guard chuckled. "Wouldn't do to have just anyone wandering in, you know."

"Oh, I see."

"Well, what are you waiting for? Go ahead, go on in. No one there yet, of course, but you can sit down inside and wait. Shouldn't be very long now." He checked his watch. "Secretaries usually start getting here in, oh, 'nother fifteen minutes."

Murray started gingerly toward the door.

"Well, be seeing you."

The door crept shut behind him. Inside was a complicated

array of offices—he could make out doorways beyond doorways—roughly in the shape of an L. He was standing in a large, high-ceilinged waiting room at the bend of the L. The room's furniture consisted of two straight-backed chairs, a worn leather couch, and two huge desks, each bearing a covered typewriter; bookcases, in a state of considerable disarray, lined the walls, which were a dispiriting shade of beige. Two windows provided generous illumination, and though they were grime-clouded, outside he could see the opposite wall of an interior courtyard, on which the morning sun was just beginning to block in the outline of roof pipes and bunkers.

Curatorial assistant. Taking a seat on the couch, he repeated the title to himself. It had sounded good enough when he said it to his friends. They didn't have to know it was the lowest position the Met had to offer—at least to an art historian. It was so low, in fact, that its holders weren't even listed on the masthead of the monthly Museum *Bulletin*. Still, it was *some*thing.

Murray took a deep breath. Was he putting his foot in it again? Should he really have taken this job? Was he ready for it? Or not. Had Chandler given him a bum steer?

When the offer had come in the mail three weeks ago Alan Chandler seemed the logical person to ask for advice. Not that there was any chance of getting an unbiased opinion out of him. The idea was even a little amusing. Impartiality was about the last thing in the world to be expected from a man who had left the employ of the Metropolitan the way he had.

Alan had been a childhood friend of Ira Murray, Roger's older brother (whose hospitality Roger was taking advantage of until he could find an apartment of his own in New York). But recently, their sojourns at Harvard having overlapped by two years, Alan had become closer to Roger. For the past year, up until about a month ago, Chandler had occupied the position of associate curator at the Met. What a story! In graduate school he'd been what is known as a "hotshot," one of those who are swiftly sized up as professorial timber and who, even before they get off a dissertation, have published acute journal articles that earn them offers from major museums and universities. But Chandler was not only brilliant, he was also fearless. Most prospective art historians, once they find out their theses must cover virgin territory (or at least present a new answer to an old question), drift into pre-Columbian burial art or Byzantine calligraphy. The gallons of ink that have flowed in the names of Monet and Corot have persuaded more than one Ph.D. candidate to look more favorably on Corsican mosaics of the third century. But Chandler was different: he had it, and he knew he had it, and, by God, he was interested in nineteenth century French painting. Before his dissertation (which turned out to be a knockout in art criticism circles) he'd written several pieces on Monet—"post–Meyer Schapiro," they were termed—and these articles somehow came to the attention of people who counted at the Metropolitan. Evidently in quite a state, they dashed him off a letter. When he got it, Chandler seemed pleased but not ecstatic. They were as fortunate (weren't they?) to find him as he was to find them. Well, Roger thought, a certain bravado was pardonable. After all, it was nearly the truth.

It was the same honesty that proved his undoing at the Met. He plunged into the job with gusto. He grew attached to Cézanne and wrote more papers. Heads nodded vigorously, but at the same time there was a small pocket of resentment against him building in the department of European paintings. His tireless attitude toward his work had aroused the suspicion that he was out for the jobs of the other curators. Nothing could have been further from the truth. Chandler himself, thoroughly immersed in scholarship, was totally blind to intradepartmental politics. For all his forthrightness he was often very obtuse about recognizing the motives of others. With a naïveté that bordered on the pathetic, he supposed that museum curators—like factory workers—were judged solely on the basis of output.

Eight months after he'd started working for the Metropolitan, the chairman of the department of European paintings resigned, and the administration, perhaps making good on some old debts, appointed a man named Gould to fill the post. Chandler was furious. His work so far had been of a high enough order to have attracted notice from as far away as London. It was nothing less than incomprehensible to him that they could have picked Gould over himself. A new man from the outside, possibly, but Gould, no. For there were two members of the European paintings staff whom Chandler regarded as beyond salvation: one was a woman named Thalia Reynolds and the other was Oscar B. (for Brewster) Gould. These two subscribed to a brand of metaphysical criticism that Chandler labeled "mystic lunacy." "They can't look at Monet's haystacks," he'd written to Murray, who was still in Cambridge at the time, "without seeing breasts (even when there's just one haystack!) or at those blackbirds above van Gogh's wheatfields without seeing the coming of Doom—when they're really in a good mood, the coming of the Second World War."

Less than ten minutes after word of Gould's promotion reached Chandler he was in the Director's office submitting his resignation, letting the Director have it with both barrels. But he didn't want to exhaust his ammunition: Gould's office was his next stop. He found the chairman-elect examining some slides he'd made on a recent trip to the Louvre. Entrance noises and a faint cough having failed to tear Gould away from his trophies, Chandler slammed a fist violently on the desk top, thereby—according to his own subsequent account—"causing the slides to waft gently to the floor like the petals of a daisy." He went on to give his personal blow-by-blow evaluation of Gould's work, at times quoting verbatim choice lines from his writings. As Gould listened his blood temperature zoomed, and by the end of the tirade it had scaled unknown heights. When he finally regained the use of his vocal cords his most devastating response was to order Chandler from his sight forever. "That," Alan replied, "will be a pleasure. In case nobody's ever told you before, you have bad breath." A week later Chandler gratefully left New York and returned to Cambridge, where he quickly found work with the Boston Museum of Fine Arts. There, he said, he was treated with a little respect. Also, Murray supplied, probably with a good deal of delicacy.

At any rate Roger had applied to the Met for a job while his friend was still in their good graces. But he wasn't very hopeful about his prospects. Entirely lacking in Chandler's kind of fortitude, he'd written a thesis on works by obscure students of Giotto, although his real interest was also the French Impressionists. It was the standard route of the academic coward: get your dissertation out of the way, then concern yourself with whatever you want. So Murray had casually informed the Met that if they hired him he intended to abandon Italian Renaissance art and investigate Manet.

By the time the offer came back from the Museum, Chandler had lost his job and Roger was having second thoughts. He didn't like the idea of leaving Cambridge and especially leaving his few friends who were still single—Cambridge seemed to foster bachelorhood. But Chandler's opinion on the matter, as always, was firm. Look, Alan sternly reminded him, wasn't it true that the Met had one of the finest Manet collections outside France? No doubt, Roger said, but the thing was, he wasn't absolutely positive he wanted to work in a museum in the first place. He wasn't sure he was cut out to be a scholar at all. Nonsense! Chandler said. Of course he was a scholar; he'd just gotten his degree, hadn't he? (Some reasoning, Murray thought.) And besides, he could put up temporarily at his brother's apartment till he found one of his own, eliminating the housing problem. (Ira Murray lived on East Seventy-ninth Street. What could be more convenient?)

Chandler bent over backward to minimize his own unfortunate association with the Met. Murray, for one thing, had much more tolerance for dishonesty and pretension than he did. Who didn't? Roger countered. But Chandler was no longer receiving. So what, he said, if taking the job meant—as it was bound to—paying lip service to the nonsensical theories of Oscar B. Gould, who was still chairman of the European paintings department. It was much more important for Murray to get on with his work, Gould or no Gould. So long as he avoided all mention of the name Alan Chandler he was reasonably safe. And that wouldn't be too hard.

5

Well, he thought, looking over the unadorned walls of the waiting room, he hadn't made any slips *yet*, anyway.

There were some shuffling noises from outside the office door, and Murray sprang up from the couch to attention. But he relaxed a second later when the door opened and two girls in their early twenties entered. ". . . But you'd just never know it to look at her," the one in front was saying. She was the shorter of the two and wore a Pucci dress (doubtless a copy), large hoop earrings, and mammoth, full-moon sunglasses. (Girls in New York, he recalled, dressed as though each new day was going to bring them face to face with Mr. Right.) She jumped a little when she caught sight of Roger. "Oh, my goodness, you scared me. I thought someone had broken in." She inspected him somewhat rudely. "You don't *look* like you've broken in, though. Does he, Dor?"

The other girl said "No" in a sober voice. She wore glasses also but it was clear that no special care had gone into their selection, and removing them probably wouldn't improve her looks.

"And not the cleaning man . . ." said the first girl. "I've got it—you're with the CIA." She paused. "No . . . no, he looks much too frightened and unsure of himself."

Strangely her comment had dispelled that feeling. He introduced himself. "I'm just starting work today."

"My name's Sandy Janis," said the shorter, more lively one. "That's Doris Corman."

Doris grunted. She was already settling down at her desk, one of the two large ones in the reception room.

"Doris is very S-E-R-I-O-U-S," Sandy said in a stage whisper.

Doris grunted again and started fishing in her handbag for something which turned out to be a compact. Letting her glasses hang by a chain that joined the earpieces, she stared into it expectantly.

Sandy gave Roger a knowing look, and he noticed that *her* handbag was the kind from which it seemed she could pull a rabbit if she wanted. "Well," Sandy said, "you've come at the right time anyway. I guess you know we're about to purchase a very big Cézanne. One of the astronomical kind. You know,

6

big deal in the papers, special exhibit in the main lobby *avec* armed guards, the whole works."

"Oh, really? I hadn't heard about it."

"You haven't—?" she began. "Oh, say, listen, Mr. Murray—"

"Roger."

"Listen, Roger, you've got to keep wide awake every minute if you expect to stay employed around *here*. Keep your nose to the ground."

"Grindstone."

"Excuse me?" She blinked.

"Nose to the grindstone. *Ear* to the ground."

"Mmm. Now the truth is, if we'd been a little quicker on the draw we might have gotten this picture for a lot less than we're going to have to pay now, let me tell you."

"The Museum hasn't bought it yet?"

"It's going up for auction next Wednesday, week from tomorrow. Does the name James Aldeburg mean anything to you?"

Murray made a helpless face.

Sandy slapped her forehead. "Listen, he's this terrifically rich millionaire—"

"Most of them are," Doris said to her typewriter.

"He's this terrifically rich millionarie," Sandy began again, with added determination, "—or at least he was."

"He died."

"About three weeks ago. And left everything to his wife. But confidentially, I don't think she's too bright. And I know for a fact she has no taste in art."

"How did you figure that one out?"

"Get this, Doris—a real questioning mind. Oh, Mr. Emerson's going to like you, kid. Well anyway, Mrs. Aldeburg— either she has no taste or she's a very easy mark because what happened was, this dealer Albert Fischer—maybe you've heard of him; he doesn't have the best reputation in the art world—Albert Fischer swoops down, literally swoops, and grabs off the picture from her at bargain prices, the poor thing."

"Poor? How much do you think she got for it?"

7

"Well, the article only said, 'for a price reported to be in excess of seven hundred thousand dollars.' "

"I wouldn't call that subsistence level."

"It's worth *much* more. *We'll* probably have to pay over a million for it. Besides, I really feel poor Mrs. Aldeburg deserves something for the way her husband treated her before he died."

"Played around right up to the very end," Doris put in musically.

"Of course you hear all sorts of rumors about people like that." Murray was a born smoother-over.

But Doris wasn't to be contradicted. "These weren't rumors," she said darkly.

"Well, as I was saying," Sandy continued, "Mrs. Aldeburg sold the picture to this Fischer character, and now it's going up for auction. You see, Fischer's is one of those dealers where they only sell by auction. So it'll probably go for over a million; there are other parties interested besides the Museum."

"A million? Which picture is it? I've probably seen it."

"If you have, you're only one of about five in the whole world. You should have read this article. Aldeburg was a little, you know, eccentric. They say he gave quite a bit to some of these far-right groups, but that's beside the point, I suppose. The main thing is, he had this stupendous collection of *objets d'art*, but he never let a soul see them. Some people said his things had been stolen, and that was why. Maybe some of them were, I don't know. In any case, the word is he has—had—an amazing lot of stuff—Picasso, Monet, Cézanne, Degas, a few older people too. It still isn't known just what he had because his widow is keeping the lid closed on everything. Out of respect for his memory or something, I guess."

"But what about the Cézanne?"

"That she's selling—just to keep out from under living expenses."

"I mean, do they think *that's* stolen?"

"Oh no. She'd never take a chance like that. The Cézanne's completely documented. Aldeburg got it at an auction in

8

Paris in 1920. Before that it was in the collection of Renoir—no less. After he died his estate was divided. Anyway, since then, maybe three people in the world have seen the picture besides Aldeburg himself, and one of them's his wife—excuse me, his widow—who wouldn't know a Cézanne from a Max Schwartz, if you ask me."

"Max Schwartz?"

"Guy who painted our apartment last summer. That's why she's getting rid of the Cézanne, you see. Means nothing to her. On the other hand, she really digs portraits of Lincoln and U. S. Grant and Andrew Jackson."

"Seven hundred thousand is still an awful lot for an unknown picture."

"It's a very big canvas. One of his last, too. Listen, we're just falling over ourselves here to get ahold of it." She paused a moment. "At least, some of us are."

"I take it not everyone's in favor."

"You take it right, kid. Mr. Emerson's having fits. You see, he doesn't believe a museum should go in for all this notoriety. You remember 'Aristotle Contemplating the Bust of Homer'? Well, Mr. Emerson said it was a great picture all right, but why did we have to make a circus act out of it? Everyone came to the Museum, but they came to see two point five million dollars, not a great painting."

"But there was no way to get it for less," Murray said.

"Just what Mr. Ferris told him. Of course, Mr. Ferris wasn't here when we bought it, but they've been having this running argument for the last few months about it. Emerson's afraid the Cézanne's going to be another 'Aristotle' and Mr. Ferris keeps saying you can't get good pictures without paying through the nose. And that means publicity. They never settle anything between them."

"This Mr. Ferris—is he new here?" Just before Murray left Cambridge there had been a briefing session with Chandler. Making no pretense at objectivity—it would have been futile—Alan went into great detail about the personalities and idiosyncrasies of the members of the European paintings department. Afterward he told what little he knew of some of the other major figures in the Museum, winding up with the Director, about whom a great deal of third- and fourth-hand information was constantly circulating. But nowhere in the description had there been mention of a Ferris.

"He's been here three or four months. He'd been considered for a job before, but the department was filled. He took the place of a man named Chandler, who resigned when he didn't get a promotion. A bit headstrong, this Chandler, though I sort of liked him myself. Kind of a bull-in-a-china-shop type, if you know what I mean." Roger had to smile at the appraisal. Meanwhile a thought occurred to Sandy. "Why?" she asked. "I mean, why did you think Ferris was new?"

"Oh . . . um . . . you said something about him not being here when the Museum bought the Rembrandt."

"Oh."

"But this man Chandler," Roger said, unable to resist the irony of the situation. "Why exactly did he resign? Most people I know aren't in the habit of quitting just because they don't get promoted."

"Well, as I said, he was very headstrong. Also, he was a real whizz, and what's more, I think he knew it. There's nothing really wrong with that. I mean, if there's anything I hate, it's false modesty. But anyway he got into a fight with the Director *and* Mr. Gould. I guess that was too much for them to bear. I still don't completely understand it, though. If *I* had been the Director, I can tell you, I'd never have let him go. He's really going to make a name for himself someday. I think, right now, he's up in Boston somewhere working for a museum."

"Well, at least he got another job."

"Damn!" This was from Doris, who was already needing her typing eraser.

"Time to get down to work," Sandy said, and swished off her coat. There followed a short ritual of hair-primping and dress-smoothing before she plopped down in her own chair at the desk next to Doris's.

"I suppose this is a pretty good job," Murray said to her.

Proclamations to the contrary notwithstanding, she clearly wasn't all ready to begin the day's work.

"Not bad. It was either this or being a secretary in an art book publisher's. A B.A. doesn't get you very much these days."

"You have a B.A.?"

"Listen to him, Dor. He thinks we're barely literate. Have I got news for you, kid. Without a B.A. you wouldn't be able to clean the floors in this place, and *with* one they just might let you take out the garbage. *If* you majored in art history. You know how many secretaries there are in Manhattan? Neither do I, but I bet ninety percent of them have been to college."

"Pretty soon you'll need a B.A. to graduate from high school."

"That's what I like about you, kiddo, you catch on fast. Now why don't you just sit down on the couch over there and wait for Mr. Emerson. He usually gets in about ten, and if I were you, I'd treasure the next forty-five minutes. They may be the last free ones you get while you're working here."

Murray picked up a copy of *Art News* and reseated himself.

At ten past ten there was a rumbling outside the door. It opened by degrees and a stringy man with horn-rimmed glasses peered in through the crack as if unfamiliar with what lay inside, then entered noisily. While he was positioning his coat on the hat tree by the door—with a care that seemed to insure its falling off before the day was out—he noticed Roger, once again springing to his feet. "Ah, yes," said the man in a tired voice, "you must be Murray. Follow me, follow me." Without looking behind him he headed for one of the adjoining offices. "My name's Emerson."

Once in the room that was plainly his own, Mr. Emerson hefted the large briefcase he was carrying onto the desk by the window. "That one over there's yours," he said, motioning to another, smaller and not so well-lit desk in a corner.

Murray looked not at the desk but at Mr. Emerson. One button of his suit was dangling by a thread and the lining of the jacket drooped below the hem in spots. The briefcase had been much repaired by adhesive and Mystic tape around the seams. There could be no question that this was the man Chandler had painted in the briefing session. Born of an aristocratic family with a long history of devoting itself to education in a spirit of noblesse oblige, Emerson had a grandfather who had taught classics at Columbia in the 1890's, a time when one prerequisite to a teaching career was an independent income. But, since then, the family had constantly sold its property, dipped into capital, and generally managed its financial affairs clumsily, so that the present Mr. Emerson's generation was forced to depend on salaries for its livelihood. Emerson's life, like the briefcase, seemed to be a series of battles against long odds to save what was left.

His private life also, according to Chandler, was beginning to fray around the edges. On the basis of overheard phone calls to and from Mrs. Emerson (who rarely put in an appearance at the Museum), Chandler decided that the marriage was heading for the rocks. The one time Emerson had discussed the problem with Alan it came out that Mrs. Emerson did a good deal of traveling, almost none of it with her husband, and got a kick out of making expensive long-distance phone calls along the way and charging them to her husband's private number. What she did on these trips no one knew, including Emerson, but a large number of people were willing to take a guess.

Mr. Emerson was standing in the center of his office, surveying it too as if for the first time. "Christ," he said, "I thought—I THOUGHT SOMEONE WAS GOING TO CLEAN UP THESE SHELVES."

"Guarantee it'll be done today, Mr. Emerson," came Sandy's voice from the outer office. "Sorry, I just couldn't get it done yesterday. I was piled over with work, completely piled over."

"Makes it sound as though she were lying in the bottom of a latrine," Emerson remarked to Murray. "Well, now, as soon as I can get a few things straightened out on the desk here, we'll go over some of the basic truths every young man at the Metropolitan should know." He started rummaging through the mire of printed matter that coated the desk top. Picking up a mimeographed sheet, he said, "Oh, Murray, while I'm getting things in order you might go outside and ask Miss Janis if she'd be good enough to get Mr. Gould on my extension. He and Mr. Ferris met with the purchasing committee yesterday. I suppose you've heard about the Cézanne we're interested in."

"It's a late work, isn't it?"

Emerson's straightening-up operations halted abruptly. "I think before we go any further we should get something straight: I'm one person around here you don't have to bother trying to impress. I hope that's entirely clear. I've read your work; it's quite . . . adequate. Well, good, now that that's all settled, could you . . ." He motioned toward the reception room.

Murray relayed Mr. Emerson's message to Sandy, but she was just hanging up the receiver, having already tried Gould. A very wide-awake girl, Murray was beginning to notice. She picked up the phone again and got Emerson's extension. "Mr. Gould's not in yet, Mr. Emerson."

"Keep trying him," Emerson said, in a voice that rendered the telephone connection superfluous. "Let me know the minute you get him. Murray!"

With renewed sympathy for yo-yos, Murray went back inside.

"Now mostly what you'll be doing," Emerson explained when Roger had taken a chair, "is research for articles we've been asked to do, reports to the administration, and editing on pieces for the various Museum publications." He plunged into a detailed outline of office procedure in the European paintings department. He'd entered into a discussion of registering and cataloguing processes, which were handled by the Registrar's office downstairs, when he caught sight of something on the floor and stopped in mid-sentence. "Damn," he said. Then: "Miss Janis!"

"Yes, Mr. Emerson." Her tone suggested that it was all she could do to concentrate on her work and keep track of his whims at the same time.

"Correct me if I'm wrong, but I believe I asked you one week ago today to remove this carton of Mr. Chandler's effects from my office."

"I know you did, Mr. Emerson, but I don't know what to do with it. Mr. Gould had it in his office for three weeks before you got it. And before that—"

"Never mind. Just see that it gets removed from here when you do the shelves—this afternoon."

"But where should I—"

"Why don't you try Mr. Ferris's office. I don't think he's logged any time with it yet."

"Yes, Mr. Emerson."

"No, Mr. Emerson." A pudgy man with a cherubic face had materialized in the office. Like everyone else, he wore the standard gray suit, but he'd let himself go in the selection of shoes. They were the kind with ornate buckles and punched borders around the leather components. It was as if his natural flamboyance, bottled up by the rest of his clothes, had trickled out his pants legs. He had discreetly long sideburns, which also added a touch of distinction to his appearance. "Morning, George. I gather this is our new curatorial assistant."

Emerson said, "Roger Murray, Stanley Ferris," and left it at that.

"Now about that box," Ferris said. "Can't have it in *my* office. Clutter up the place." He grinned. "Have to keep things neat." His style was breezy; Murray put him down as the sort whose perpetual good humor often evokes homicidal feelings in those around him.

"I forgot," Emerson said. "I wish you'd let me in on your secret sometime, Stanley. How you manage to keep your desk so clean. I put something away, and right off something new grows in its place. Sort of like the five hundred hats of Bartholomew Cubbins."

"Hmm?"

"Dr. Seuss. Not your style at all. When you were little you probably read Proust."

"But in translation, of course." He smiled again. Then he

14

became solemn. "Well, Gould and I saw the purchasing committee yesterday, George."

"And?"

"They're dying to get the Aldeburg Cézanne. Not sure how high they're prepared to go on it, but I got the feeling—don't quote me—that they'd okay a million and a half. At least, if they don't, we're not going to take the bidding. Naturally, they were constantly reminding everyone of how much we've been spending recently."

"Don't look at me. I was against the Monet, if you remember."

"Believe me, George, you're about the last person in the world they blame. In fact, I got the feeling that your, shall we say, economic prudence has ingratiated you tremendously with the trustees. No, *I'm* the one they shout at. But what I say is, if you want high-quality stuff—"

"—you have to pay. I know."

"You're too cynical. At least it gets people into the Museum. People who would stay home otherwise get exposed to great art."

"Maybe they'd be better off staying home. Excuse me." The phone in front of Emerson had rung once and one of its buttons was flashing. He picked it up and said into the mouthpiece, "Emerson . . . Yes . . . Put him on . . . Oh, good morning, Mr. Fischer . . ."

Ferris gave Murray an appreciative nod.

". . . Fine, and you? . . . Yes, I'm listening . . . Was *what*? . . . Well, how did it happen? What's missing?"

At these last words both Ferris's and Murray's eyes flew to Mr. Emerson and stayed there as if under the sway of a powerful magnet.

There was a long pause. Finally, Mr. Emerson said into the receiver, "I see . . . Yes . . . Everything's under control now, though . . . Right . . . Listen, I think I'll ask one of our people to drop by your place, just to get a first-hand picture . . . Fine . . . Thank you for letting us know . . . Good-bye." He hung up the phone and clasped his hands in front of him on the desk.

15

"For Christ's sake, George, don't keep us in suspense," Ferris said.

"Someone broke into Fischer's last night," Emerson answered calmly.

"What!" said Murray.

"Oh my God!" said Ferris.

"Now take it easy. The Cézanne's safe."

Ferris sighed elaborately. "You mean someone got in to Fischer's gallery and left the Cézanne *alone*? Why? What was the point?"

"Don't ask me. Fischer wasn't exactly coherent over the phone just now. But he did say something about the Cézanne being hidden away in a back room."

"Well, what the hell did they break in for? What did they take?"

"A few things by some nineteenth century Americans, though who would want paintings by nineteenth century Americans is more than I can fathom."

"Did they do any damage? I mean, what *happened*?"

"Listen, don't get excited, Stanley. I'm going to see if I can get Oscar again. I tried him earlier but he wasn't in yet. Not like him to be late, though. I think we should send someone over there just to check up—on the condition of the Cézanne if nothing else." Emerson picked up the phone again and asked Sandy to try Gould's office. A few seconds later he put it down once more. "Still not here. That's very strange, don't you think?"

"Maybe they called him at his home and he's already over there."

"No, I think Fischer would have said something about it." He sighed. "Well, I guess I'm elected to go down there. And just when I've got all this—" He stopped. "I have an idea. Murray, your first official function on behalf of the Metropolitan will be to go over to Albert Fischer's gallery and check out the situation. Tell him I'll be around to see him later in the day. Oh, and on your way out, would you ask Miss Janis to keep trying Mr. Gould." To himself he added, "Not like Oscar, not like him at all," and shook his head.

"I heard," Sandy said, before Roger could repeat the message. "Mr. Emerson is under the impression you have to say everything a hundred times to a secretary before it sinks in."

"I think you should be a little more tolerant," Roger said. "Hmm?"

"Nothing. Better be on my way."

"Too bad you're going to miss the fun at this end. I have a sneaking suspicion it's going to be one of those days."

TWO

THE FISCHER GALLERY, as it was formally known, was on the second floor of an austere sandstone building on Madison Avenue in the lower Seventies. To get to the exhibition rooms visitors had to take an elevator that let them off inside the gallery itself—it occupied the entire second floor—but before that they had to pass muster with a sequence of uniformed officials: a doorman, a lobby superintendent, an elevator operator, and finally a secretary behind a reception desk before the entrance to the exhibition rooms.

Murray had been to galleries but never to one of this magnitude. Expecting splendor, he was mildly disappointed. The exhibition rooms were lined with large oriental rugs that were not only dirty but also threadbare—to the extent that the underlay embarrassingly showed through in patches. The walls too were dirty, and the paint was starting to crack at the tops. "Fischer's money is so old," Chandler had once said, "that he doesn't have it anymore," a reference to the fact that the Fischer family had made their money in the nineteenth century, as against some of the other art gallery owners whose treasury notes were considerably crisper.

18

On the walls were paintings dazzling in their diversity, if not in their individual quality. An elegant Sisley and a picture whose signature Murray had to investigate to make sure it wasn't the work of his Uncle Herman were neighbors. Beneath the paintings was a no less uneven display of antique furniture, and the total effect was of someone who knew a great deal about art but didn't know what he liked.

"May I help you?" said a paunchy man in a white shirt, bow tie, and beige cable-stitch cardigan sweater. His hair was combed straight back and overhung the collar of his shirt in the rear by about an inch. He wore glasses with thick eye-distorting lenses, and a short cigar seemed as much a part of his appearance as the glasses. This had to be Albert Fischer himself, if only because it was well known that a certain thrifty streak had led the gallery owner to hire a minimum of professional help.

Fischer's words had brought home to Murray for the first time his ignorance of the true purpose of this visit. "Well," he said tentatively, "I'm from the Metropolitan Museum. I'm, uh, Mr. Emerson's new curatorial assistant."

"Yes?" Fischer's lips rolled over the cigar.

"He sent me over here to find out what happened last night. We heard someone broke in and—"

This was enough to set the gallery owner off. "Broke in, you're telling *me*! You realize they could have taken everything I own! They had their pick. It's a miracle they didn't take any more then they did. A miracle, that's what it is. I don't know what I'm going to do." He put his palms to his forehead theatrically.

"But you're insured, of course."

Cold comfort. "Insured? What's *insured*? Naturally, everything's insured. You think the insurance would cover it? My friend, this is an auction gallery. We sell to the highest bidder. I've practically never had a single piece go through here that didn't sell for twice its insured value."

"But I thought only two small pictures were taken. We heard it was almost nothing."

"Almost nothing. What's almost nothing? No, they didn't

19

take the Cézanne. You think I'd be here this morning—alive —if they did? It's what they *could* have taken. They could have taken anything; they had their pick. Oh, my blood pressure!"

Murray allowed a few seconds for Mr. Fischer's blood pressure to sink and his rate of breathing to return to normal. "Why do you suppose they left the Cézanne?"

"Why? Who knows why? Who knows why anybody steals? They've got twisted minds is why. And with a twisted mind who knows why people do anything?"

"But I mean," Murray said, trying to steer the conversation back to the realm of logic, "did you have the picture in a vault where they couldn't get at it?"

"No, no, I didn't." He was beginning to calm down. "I didn't want to put the Cézanne in there because I was worried about damage. You see, I'm getting some temperature-and-humidity-control equipment put in in there, but it hasn't come yet. This is special equipment, the very latest thing, in addition to what we have for the rest of the gallery. So I didn't want to take the chance with the Cézanne. I left it in the back, in a room with a special lock on the door hooked up to the burglar alarm system."

"Then they never saw the Cézanne."

"Who knows? The door was open this morning when I came in."

"*What*? You mean someone did get in there?"

"Maybe and maybe not. You see, I have this burglar alarm system with an electric-eye type gadget. You step across the beam and *wham*—bells ring, lights go on, something even goes off down in the police station. And I got cameras too, movie cameras, start going as soon as anyone breaks in. Automatically. Just like a bank. But when the system's off all the locks are unlocked. Anyone can just walk in."

"They must have turned the thing off then."

"Listen, the Museum got a real smart boy in you." Teeth showed around the cigar.

"But how did they do it?"

"How? he asks. Don't ask. They first of all took out the

fuse for the burglar alarm system. Now this fuse box is closed in such a way that it only opens when a fuse burns out. Otherwise I can't even open it. So what they must have done, they must have burned out the fuse for the *lights*—from the outside—so the box would open automatically. That disconnects everything. Then they slugged my night guard over the head and just walked in. They slugged a couple other guards too. May their hands grow thorns—on the *inside!*"

"So they *could* have taken the Cézanne. Why do you think they didn't?"

"Maybe they couldn't find it, I don't know. Maybe they were worried what would happen if they got caught with it. Just be thankful they *didn't* take it."

"It seems they went to a lot of work for just two small pictures, though. Did the police check to see if anyone had been back there and *saw* the Cézanne?"

"What can the police tell? There were no fingerprints, of course not; the thieves wore gloves. Look, they watch television too, you know."

"What about footprints?" Roger asked, for want of a more sensible question.

"Footprints? Who can tell? There were thousands of them back there. Loads of people been in that room."

"A lot of people have seen the picture since you got it?"

"Oh no, but I kept other things back there. I just brought the Cézanne in yesterday, and quite a production to get it here, let me tell you. Only two people in the whole day yesterday to see it. Both from your museum, as a matter of fact: Mr. Gould and Mr. Ferris. You see, I gotta be careful who I take back there. Only take people who really might be interested in buying. And I take them *personally.* Nobody else allowed into the room without me along with 'em."

"Mr. Gould and Mr. Ferris were the only people who came yesterday? Why doesn't the rest of the department come over?"

"They will, they will. For a picture this important everybody over there'll have to take a look at it. The rest of them'll be here today. Mr. Emerson's coming, Miss Reynolds too, and that Mrs. Mayer. Listen, I know them all, every one," Fischer said stubbornly.

"What about other collectors?"

"They'll be here too, you don't have to worry. I've got a list of appointments for today long as your arm."

Murray involuntarily inspected his arm. "Well, Mr. Emerson should be over this afternoon. I should be getting back, I guess."

"Give him my warmest regards," said Fischer, and Murray had some difficulty determining how the message had been intended.

Outside on Madison Avenue again, Roger pulled the lapels of his suit jacket together against the wind—he'd been too lazy to bring his coat—and reflected on the events of the day so far. If his brother Ira asked him tonight what kind of day he'd had, Roger would be hard pressed to describe it. He went over to a gallery to question the owner about a robbery there the night before? What are you, Ira would be certain to ask—an art critic or a policeman? And just what had he learned at Fischer's? Practically nothing; he hadn't even gotten a look at the Cézanne. Was Emerson going to quiz him on its condition? He had a sudden impulse to race back upstairs and ask to see the picture. But a lot of good that would do, he decided, and chose instead to stop in at a drugstore he was just passing, through whose window he'd noticed a soda fountain.

It was a little before one by the time Murray arrived back at the offices of the European paintings department. He'd dawdled over lunch, stopped in to see the new exhibit at the Whitney (lightproof boxes in which you walked around feeling the sculpture), and tried (in vain) to pick up a girl on his way out. Nevertheless, he'd managed to arrive back at the Museum before any of the other members of the department. Anticipating a few comfortable minutes on the reception room couch, he was about to hunt around for something to read when the door slammed behind him and a craggy, jowly woman of about fifty entered. Unmindful of any other presence in the room, she stabbed the mother-of-pearl-handled umbrella she was carrying into an umbrella stand next to the hat tree by the door, *clunk*. Murray stole a glance out the window, but no sudden shower had spring up in the last ten minutes while he wasn't looking.

"Oh, dear," the woman said, noticing—but apparently not addressing—Roger. To him she announced: "I'm sorry, no visitors allowed in here. You'll have to leave immediately; this is strictly personnel."

"I *am* personnel," Murray said, feeling eminently ridiculous.

The woman thawed only a degree or two. "I don't believe I've had the pleasure." She fumbled in a severe black handbag and drew out a pair of glasses, which she briskly installed. "In fact, I'm sure I don't know you. Who are you?"

"Roger Murray, the new—"

"Of course, of course, of course—the new curatorial assistant, I remember. Very pleased to meet you, I'm Miss Reynolds."

Ah yes, Chandler had warned him about Thalia Reynolds. "In this life," Chandler had said in one of his mock-philosophic moods, "some of us are yachts, some of us are tugboats, and some of us are ocean liners. Miss Reynolds is an ice-breaker." The door slam and umbrella clunk, often accompanied by a cataclysmic throat-clearing, were her self-performed fanfare. Radcliffe, '42, she was aging with enthusiasm, accentuating the gray in her hair, it was rumored, rather than obliterating it. She wore the same navy blue suit day in and day out, signed her name illegibly, and, most curious of all, had a gift Chandler referred to as "absolute calendar." It was a talent similar to absolute pitch; whereas a person with absolute pitch can tell you blindfolded that a certain musical note is a G, Thalia Reynolds could tell you offhand that a certain date three months away was a Thursday. To some she was a formidable figure. To Chandler she was "the other know-nothing of the department"—besides Gould. And, if it could be imagined, she was even more dogmatic about her views than the chairman.

"I'm told you went over to see the Cézanne this morning," she said. "There was some kind of disturbance or other at Fischer's, so I've heard."

"I did go over there, yes," Murray said, "but I didn't get to see the painting."

"You didn't? Might I ask why not?"

Murray looked over in the direction of the office door on the chance it might be about to open. "Well . . . I did go over to make sure there was no damage, but Mr. Fischer assured me—"

"Mr. Fischer assured you? Mr. Fischer assured you? Is that the best you can do? My heavens, I wouldn't trust that man farther than I could throw a rhinoceros. Do you know what he did?"

Murray tore himself away from an image her words had conjured up in his mind to say "No."

"Well, I'd like you to know he practically badgered James Aldeburg's widow to death to get that picture. He was over there constantly, making a nuisance of himself, giving her not a moment's peace. I know her quite well, a fine woman. Meek." (If she was anything but a woman of steel one breath from Miss Reynolds had probably knocked her galley-west.) "She was very upset about James's death, poor woman. She only sold the painting because she couldn't bear to be reminded of her husband."

"Reminded? I thought it was a painting of a—"

"Of a bridge, yes. 'Le Pont des Trois Sautets' is the name of it, a magnificent work. But it wasn't the bridge, you know," she said, dispelling any thought he might be harboring that James Aldeburg, in life, had resembled a bridge. "It was the *thought*. It was one of his very favorite paintings. He absolutely adored it. He kept it in a room by itself, I understand, and he would go in there every night just to stare at it.

"And he never let anyone else into that room either."

Miss Reynolds was gazing off into the distance, as though by extreme effort she could penetrate the walls of the Aldeburg estate fifty miles away. "It's a very great work. I see it as a sort of spiritual affirmation."

"You've seen it then."

"Oh, no, but I'm *prepared* for it. It's the culmination of his entire art. I'm sure I won't be disappointed when I actually do get a look at it. I know what to expect; I've seen just about every other Cézanne in existence."

And very likely a few besides, Murray was thinking, when the door opened and Mr. Emerson entered.

"I've just been discussing the new Cézanne with Mr. Murray here," she informed him. "It'll be a great addition to our collection."

"I'm sorry to have to remind you it's not ours yet," Mr. Emerson pointed out, hanging up his coat. "We'll have to win the bidding first."

"But of course we'll win the bidding. We have to. You know what a painting like this does for the Museum. Think about the Rembrandt, think about the Monet, think about the Frescoes exhibit. You have to admit these things bring people into the Museum."

Murray was a little surprised to hear Mr. Emerson say, "I suppose they do," and then he recalled that Chandler considered him one of the foremost handlers of Miss Reynolds in the department. "By the way," Emerson said, "you haven't seen Oscar this morning, have you?"

"Mr. Gould? No. I thought he was speaking to the purchasing committee."

"That was last night. I can't imagine where he could be. Miss Janis has been trying his office all morning."

"Well, I'm not his private secretary, Mr. Emerson. I'm afraid my article doesn't leave me time to worry about Mr. Gould's whereabouts." Her article, Murray recalled, was something of a legend in the department. It had been in the works for years, although no one was quite sure what it was about. Chandler's conclusion, deduced from various scraps he'd uncovered, was that it was on the influence of Flemish painting on El Greco and Renoir—or at least these three subjects came into it somehow. At any rate the chances were that when one of the other members of the staff looked in on Miss Reynolds he would get, "Not now, not now, please.

25

I'm at a very critical point in my article. Would ten minutes do?" At the moment she looked over at Mr. Emerson and said, "Why don't you try him at his home?"

Emerson's eyebrows arched—advice so patently sensible from Thalia Reynolds didn't come along every day. "I think I will," he said, and shambled into his office.

"Well," said Miss Reynolds, "very nice to have met you, Mr. Morrill," and she was gone too.

Murray went inside to report to Mr. Emerson. When he got there his superior was holding the telephone receiver in his right hand and gazing at it uncomprehendingly. "Line seems to be out of order. There's just this dull hum on the wire when you dial his number. Remarkable." He carefully put the receiver down. "Listen, Murray? This is very strange, Oscar not showing up. I wonder if I could ask you a favor. I'd like you to hop over to Mr. Gould's apartment and see what the story is over there." He ran a palm down his face. "Ordinarily I wouldn't ask you a thing like this—"

"I don't mind," Murray said hastily.

"I appreciate it. Now Mr. Gould lives in a cooperative on Fifty-seventh Street. Let me give you all the information. Do you have a pencil?"

With the address on a memo pad sheet in his shirt pocket, Murray started for the door. In the reception room he ran into Ferris, who was looking for Elizabeth Mayer, an associate curator. (Was everybody around here looking for someone?) "Off again?" he said to Murray.

"Mr. Emerson's asked me to go over and see what happened to Mr. Gould. He doesn't answer his home phone; the line doesn't even ring."

"Check up on his private life, eh? Good idea. No telling what that man does with his free time. Divorced twice, you know."

"Oh, I'm . . . sorry to hear it."

"Don't be. I don't think Gould's very sorry, why should you be? In any case, let me know what you find. It's probably something very juicy." He rubbed his hands together. "I can't wait."

On his way downtown in the Number 2 Bus, Murray began to question his long-held belief that life in the art world was a dry and uneventful existence. He'd once thought it was so dry and uneventful, in fact, that in spite of his great love of line and color he'd seriously considered finding another field. Yet here he was traipsing across town to find out why the chairman of the European paintings department hadn't shown up for work this morning. While it wasn't his idea of the respected art historian's typical day—nor was it likely to set any patterns—he had to admit he was feeling no intolerable pain.

Gould lived in one of the stately old buildings on Fifty-seventh Street near Sutton Place. Each window had a marble ledge beneath it, and the windows themselves were mullioned. Owing to extreme age, their panes reflected the light unevenly. Beneath a green canvas canopy that spanned the sidewalk in front of the main entrance stood a stiff doorman who nodded sedately to residents of the building and all but blocked the doorway to anyone else.

Murray was allowed through, but only after coughing up Gould's full name and apartment number. The apartment itself was on the fourth floor, and he instructed the tiny, gum-chewing, pink and white elevator man to take him there. At first the man gave no sign of having heard, but several seconds later he lackadaisically tossed the car door closed and flipped the control handle, producing a stomach-bouncing lurch. During the trip he worked his gum with his jaw two or three times per floor, as if the chewing was essential to the elevator's progress.

At Four, Murray got off and walked uneasily down the hallway, which was carpeted in faded zebra-stripe broadloom. He stopped in front of 4 D, pressed the bell, and while he was waiting noticed, by means of a covert sidelong glance, that the elevator operator had made no move to take the car back down again but was leaning against the elevator door frame watching him with the small degree of embarrassment he might exhibit at observing actors on a screen. Murray rang the bell again and waited, humming and patting his hands against his sides. After another twenty seconds or so he tried again. The bell was working; he could hear its buzz. He tried a fourth time.

Well, he'd done all he could. If Emerson wasn't satisfied, let *him* come over and try.

"No answer, huh?" said the elevator man as Murray came back down the hallway.

"You haven't by any chance seen Mr. Gould today?" Murray asked. "Four D?"

The small man noisily and deliberately exacted some juice from his gum in three well-defined scrunches before answering. "Nope."

"Did he go out at all today? Were you on duty the whole time?"

Another scrunch. "Since six this morning, pal. He gone out, I seen him."

"Did you see him yesterday?" Murray tried.

"Ain't here Mondays. Day off."

"Well, did anyone see him? He must have come back home from work."

"Smatterofact, the other fella happened to tell me he saw Mr. Gould come in. Seems Mr. Gould wanted this other fella to be on the lookout in case another apartment in the building came vacant. Was shopping around for a bigger place, y' know. Other fella told me to be on the lookout too." As if recovering from such a lengthy bout with the language he inhaled deeply and squeezed the gum a few times in rapid succession.

"You mean he came home last night and he hasn't left the apartment since?"

"Near as I can figure, pal."

"But I just rang his bell. He doesn't answer."

"Mighta gone out by the stairs, maybe."

"Does he often do that?" Murray inquired earnestly.

"Never known him to before, but y' never know. Might be wanting the exercise."

"Wouldn't the man at the front door have seen him go out?"

"Less he went out the back, o' course."

"Does he often—Uh, who was at the front door this morning?"

The elevator man shut his eyes and smiled angelically.

"I thought you said you were running the elevator," Murray said.

"Do both till ten in the morning."

"And you didn't see him go out."

"Nope."

Roger was beginning to regard his mission in a more serious light. Until now he'd half suspected the whole trip of being a task Emerson had fobbed off on him for lack of anything more substantial to assign. But there just might be something to this. If not, why hadn't Gould left his apartment this morning? Or if he had, why sneak out? And, in any event, he should have phoned the Museum before now to let them know he wouldn't be in.

The elevator came elastically to a stop. As Murray stepped out onto the marble floor of the lobby he asked, "I wonder if there's any way you could, uh, let me into Mr. Gould's apartment. I have the feeling something's the matter."

The elevator man grinned. "Not me, nooo."

"Is there a superintendent in the building?"

"Mmm, Pratt." Scrunch.

"I beg your pardon."

"Pratt his name is, Abner Pratt."

"Would he have a key to Mr. Gould's apartment?"

"Might be he would. Have to ask him, though."

"Where would I find him?"

"Downstairs. Basement. Entrance outside in the alley."

Murray thanked the elevator man and walked out the front door. He had no trouble finding the alley, which was along the right-hand wall of the building. When he got there he saw a lanky man sweeping it out with a long-handled brush. His limbs looked as though they couldn't possibly contain bones, and he'd apparently been sick the day coordination was handed out. Altogether, with his idiotic smile, he reminded Murray of Ray Bolger as the Scarecrow in *The*

Wizard of Oz. "Something I can do for you, young man?" he said, not very amiably.

Murray got a whiff of air burdened with the combined odor of sweat and alcohol. "Are you the superintendent?" he asked.

"That's right. Pratt's the name." He leaned on the handle of the brush and waited.

"I was looking for Mr. Gould upstairs," Murray said.

"You want Mr. Gould, it's Four D, you just go up there and ring his bell, okay?"

"I tried that. He doesn't answer."

"Then you just turn right smack around and go home and come back some other time. What you bothering me for? Don't I got enough troubles with my sciatica and all? I tell you the pains—"

"Wait a second. Will you let me explain, will you just let me explain for a second? I work over at the Museum where Mr. Gould works, and he hasn't shown up today, and he hasn't called or anything to say he wouldn't be in, and, well, we're pretty worried about what might have happened to him."

"So you're worried, so big deal. What do you want me to do about it?"

"You haven't seen him today, have you?"

"No, I haven't. My sciatica don't let me get out much—"

"So that means," Murray went on inexorably, "he probably didn't leave the building at all today. Now what I thought was, maybe you could let me into Mr. Gould's apartment. You could just give me the key and let me go up there myself. You wouldn't even have to make the trip."

The superintendent shook his head a number of times. "Nothing doing. What do you think I am—crazy? I got responsibilities, friend. I can't just go around giving out keys to any party walks in off the street."

"Well, could you come with me then? It's very important."

Something, perhaps the thought of crisp new bills or a bottle of whiskey around Christmas time, changed Mr. Pratt's mind. "Aw heck, follow me," he said, and repaid Murray for the inconvenience by going into great detail, on the way back upstairs, about his sciatica. It turned out he had rheumatism too.

He was extra-careful to ring Gould's bell twice and then knock before using his pass key. "Mr. Gould?"

"Mr. Gould," Murray said, a little louder.

The two stepped inside, and Pratt trod cautiously down a hallway to the left of the front door. Murray went straight ahead into the living room. It was sumptuously decorated with such things as jade sculpture and a Chippendale lowboy.

The first hint of something out of order was the telephone. It had been thrown onto the polished wooden parquet floor, its wire ripped from the wall and the receiver separated from the dialing component by the length of the connecting cord. Murray flinched at the sight, as if it had been a small, slightly poisonous snake. Next he observed an irregularity across the room in an alcove lined with ceiling-high, richly grained teak bookshelves, all filled: the alcove had its own indirect lighting system and it was on.

But this was the middle of the day.

He timidly stepped across the oriental rug that covered the major part of the living room floor, and he could see a mahogany work table on which several books sat open. On the floor, though, most unusual of all, there was a bundle of laundry—a rather large bundle—wrapped in a silk paisley bathrobe. Now that was really strange, leaving a thing like that right out in the middle of—

Oh my God!

Murray fell back against a wall. Apparently leaking from the laundry bundle were the drying remains of a deep red stream, a stream that might very recently have been flowing.

Oh my God, oh my God, this was no laundry bundle.

"Mr.—Mr. Pratt," he finally managed to cry out, "would you come in here a minute, please?"

THREE

"THIS OSCAR GOLD MUSTA BEEN SOME HOTSY-TOTSY, they gotta close the whole Museum for him," said a matronly woman to her companion as the two of them brushed past Murray on the steps before the Metropolitan's main entrance. At the top of the steps was the customary pre-opening-bell gathering, which the women had just abandoned. This morning it seemed to be producing more than the usual hubbub, and Murray skipped up the steps to investigate. Elbowing his way through the small crowd, he saw the reason for the commotion: in front of the wooden storm shed that protects the main doors was an aluminum stand with a hand-written cardboard sign in its frame that read: *Out of respect for the memory of Oscar B. Gould, the Curator of European Paintings, this museum will be closed all day.*

The sign was Emerson's work, no doubt, Murray told himself. Now finally, he was beginning to believe in the reality of the previous afternoon's events . . .

"I've got to get out of here," Murray had said to the superintendent, who was hysterically bouncing his head around, looking from the body on the floor to Murray and back.

"Hold it a minute. HOLD IT!"

But Murray was already out the door, and scampering down a back stairway, his stomach a very unwilling party to the flight. He ran out into the street and found himself heading for Park Avenue before he started to question his destination. What was he looking for? A phone booth! he was reminded as he caught sight of one on the corner of Lexington Avenue. In his dazed condition he was almost ready to swear that the booth was trying to elude him; it looked as though it was standing there by the curb waiting for the light to change. But he managed to stumble inside and dial the Museum. When he was finally put through to European paintings, Emerson came on the line. Murray thought he recognized the voice, but he wasn't taking any chances. "Mr. Emerson?"

"Yes . . ." Emerson clearly hadn't the faintest idea who it was.

"Mr. Emerson, this is Roger Murray."

"Oh, yes, Murray. Where are you? I thought you were coming straight back here after you stopped by Mr. Gould's."

"I was, yes."

"You did go over to Mr. Gould's place, didn't you?"

Murray had something caught in his throat at this point. "What's that?"

"I said, I did. I went over there."

"And?"

"Mr. Emerson . . . something . . . something's happened to Mr. Gould . . ."

"Stop playing games, Murray. I knew something had happened. Why do you think I sent you over there?"

The words rushed out: "Mr. Emerson, Mr. Gould's dead."

There was an interval of faraway electronic humming from the earpiece. Then: "What did you say?"

"Mr. Gould's dead. Shot, I think."

"Dead? Shot? What are you talking about? You mean he's sick or something?"

With a vague memory that in ancient Egypt (or somewhere) they had executed messengers who imparted unwelcome tidings, Murray became frenzied. "Mr. Emerson, I'm trying to tell you, Mr. Gould's been murdered. Shot. Dead. The police are going to have to be called, there's going to have to be an investigation, there's going to be . . ."

"Murray, are you all right?"

"I'm fine. No, I'm not, but this is all *true*. I was just over there."

"But he was in the office yesterday. . . . He couldn't be . . ." Slowly, he was getting his bearings back. "Murray, did you say you hadn't called the police yet?"

"Yes. I mean, no, I haven't called them. I rushed out of there to call you. I haven't spoken to anyone except the superintendent of the building."

"All right, listen. I'll call the police. You go back there now, to Mr. Gould's building. And, Murray?"

"I'm still here."

"The Museum may be closed tomorrow. I'll have to tell the Director. He may want to close. But you get all the details now, and come in tomorrow anyway. I'll be here. Do you understand that?"

"I think so . . ."

Then he'd run all the way back to the building, but by the time he got there the situation was rapidly changing. Apparently someone had already called the authorities. Police cars were pulling up to the front entrance in droves, and policemen were getting out of them and swarming inside. When he got inside himself, he saw that the place was already teeming with civil servants—white-coated men connected with a hospital or possibly the morgue, plainclothes detectives, police photographers and fingerprint men, all in business suits, and plenty of the garden-variety men in blue. The last seemed to be forever springing from the walls by spontaneous generation. It was a madhouse! Soon the men of the press arrived, an agitated, pushy, obstinate contingent to whom he was allowed to speak only after the police were finished with him. *And* they knew where they could find him if they needed him . . .

He prayed they could live without him this morning and

walked back down the steps and around to the Seventy-ninth Street entrance that leads to the children's section. There he identified himself to the guard and was let through. When he opened the door of the European paintings office, things looked pretty much normal except that the door to Emerson's office was closed.

Without looking up from her typewriter, Sandy said, "You're late. The police have been here asking for you. Thought you might have skipped the country."

Roger sighed. "I got about an hour's sleep last night. I just can't take this kind of thing." He indicated Mr. Emerson's door. "What's with him this morning?"

"They're in there now."

"The police?"

She nodded. "They're interviewing everybody separately so there won't be any, quote, collusion."

"Collusion?"

"Miss Reynolds is demanding to see her lawyer before she says a word."

"Well," Murray said, "I've already told them all I know. They won't need to speak to me."

"I wouldn't be too sure of that." Mr. Emerson's door had opened and a narrow-eyed, middle-aged man was standing in the doorway. What struck Murray even more forcibly than the eyes, which were two straight black slits, was the neck, which was conspicuously lacking. His chin reposed squarely on the knot of his tie. "You're Roger Murray, is that right? Lieutenant Sugrue, homicide division."

Murray mumbled a greeting.

"I realize you've already given us a statement, Mr. Murray," Sugrue said. "But we need a few more details from you. You understand." He smiled thinly, and it was plain that smiling was not an activity he came by naturally.

"Take him for as long as you need," Emerson said with irony that was lost on his listener. "I'd like to offer you the premises of my office for the interview, but I'm afraid I'm expecting some people in very shortly, and there's no place else we can go."

35

"Don't mention it," Lieutenant Sugrue said, wheeling out another thin smile. "I thought we might just take a stroll around the Museum. It's my understanding you're closed to the public for the day."

"That's correct."

"Well, I hope you don't mind, Mr. Murray. Why don't you lead the way."

Roger opened the office door for him, and the two started out toward the front of the Museum. The lieutenant, he decided, reminded him in a vague way of Richard Nixon, although physically there was no resemblance. It was perhaps that Sugrue like the President, regarded his mission in life as one demanding perpetual sobriety. Attempts at humor required a supreme effort on his part, and usually fell flat.

In the first large gallery they came to Sugrue stopped and perused some of the paintings. "Why don't you just relax, Mr. Murray," he said, not taking his eyes from a large Manet bullfighter. "Maybe you could tell me a little about the paintings in this room. I'm always interested in artistic things."

Murray checked to make sure Sugrue wasn't kidding and then said, without enthusiasm, "The paintings in this room were done in the early and middle nineteenth century. Many of the painters belonged to what was called the Barbizon School, and the others are more properly associated with the Impressionist movement. Edouard Manet, whose pictures you see over here—"

"That's very interesting, Mr. Murray. I hate to interrupt, but I wonder if you could tell me anything about Mr. Gould. What did you think of him as a person?"

"Nothing."

"Nothing?"

"I'd never met him."

"Oh, that's right, you just started working here yesterday. Is that right?"

"I don't even know if you could count that. I didn't spend much time actually in the office yesterday."

"Oh? How was that?"

"Well, in the morning Mr. Emerson sent me over to Albert

Fischer's gallery to check up on things. They'd had a robbery the night before. And in the afternoon I was sent over to Mr. Gould's, and you know what happened there. Incidentally, while we're on the subject, I wonder if you could tell me something."

"I'll try. Assuming it's not top secret, classified." Another futile attempt at a smile.

"It's about the robbery at Fischer's. I don't understand what thieves do with stolen paintings. They can't cut them up and sell them as a lot of smaller paintings."

"That's true," Sugrue said ponderously. "Now I'm not closely connected with the people who handle art thefts, but it's my understanding what happens is, there are a lot of very rich art collectors hanging around. Very eccentric too, these people. Do anything to get their hands on original paintings even if it means having someone steal them for them. Of course, once they get a stolen painting they can't show it to anyone, but that's the price they're willing to pay. All they want is the satisfaction of having it, I suppose." He shook his head. "No shortage of nuts in the world."

"I have another question, then. These thieves who broke in to Fischer's gallery—they had their pick of anything in the place, and there was a priceless Cézanne just sitting there. Why wouldn't they have taken that?"

"Could be a lot of reasons. First of all, maybe somebody especially wanted the pictures they took. Do business on special order, these people. But most likely they couldn't have gotten away with this other picture. You see, we know pretty much who these nuts are that collect stolen paintings. Once something really big is stolen we watch them for the next few months, make sure nothing goes in or out."

"If you know who they are why don't you arrest them?"

"Can't. First of all, we'd need a search warrant to find the stuff, which might not be so easy to get. Second, they've got the stuff pretty well hidden. And third, most of them live in the South of France, where the laws are a little different. But if we catch a painting going in, we've got 'em. That's generally the only way we do get 'em."

"I see."

"Now if we could get back to Mr. Gould." Lieutenant Sugrue approached another Manet and stealthily removed a note pad from an inner pocket of his suit jacket as if he were about to record some intricacies of brushstroke. "You say you only started working here yesterday. Did you meet most of the people in the office up there?"

"Just Mr. Emerson and Mr. Ferris . . . and Miss Reynolds. And the two secretaries. I think there's another curator, Mrs. Mayer, who I haven't met yet."

"And what did you think of them? I mean, did you get any strong impressions right off?"

"Yes, I definitely thought Miss Reynolds had homicidal tendencies the moment I saw her. I'd keep a close watch on her if I were you."

"You wha—!" He relaxed. "Mr. Murray, please, I don't think this is any time for humor. We're investigating a murder."

"Sorry."

"Now can you think of any reason anyone here might have had for murdering Mr. Gould? Even in the short time you've been here you might have noticed something, something that people who've been here longer might take for granted."

"Nothing very important."

"Maybe I'd be a better judge of that. Tell me, anyway."

"Well, Mr. Emerson has a small mole on the left side of his face. Right about here, and—"

"Mr. Murray."

"I told you it wasn't very important."

"I meant," Sugrue said deliberately, "anything having a definite bearing on the murder. Now I honestly advise you to take a little more serious attitude. Especially with regard to my next question." A master of suspense, Sugrue chose this moment to head for the adjoining gallery. "Let me ask you," he said, after camping firmly in front of a small Degas, "do you know of anyone outside the Museum who might have had a motive for killing Mr. Gould?"

My God, he couldn't mean . . . "I can't think of anyone."
"Try hard."

He *did* mean . . . Chandler—who had the perfect motive! Until now Murray hadn't connected Gould's murder with his friend. But what must the police think if they knew about that business! And Emerson had of course told them about it. Still, there was no reason for the police to think Murray had anything to do with Chandler. Emerson couldn't have told them that. "There was a man named Chandler here, I understand," Murray said carefully, "but he left a few months ago. The story is he had a little unpleasantness with Mr. Gould before he resigned."

"That's the story, isn't it? You only have it second hand?"

This was entirely unexpected. What was he supposed to say? Did Sugrue have any definite information, or was he just groping? Murray couldn't be sure, but lying to the police, he suspected, was punishable by fine or imprisonment or both. "Not exactly. I'd like to say something if I could be sure Mr. Emerson wouldn't hear about it."

"You have my word, though I don't think it'll make the least bit of difference."

"Well," Murray said, observing that his shoes could use polishing. "I know Alan Chandler. He's a fairly good friend of mine, only I didn't want anyone at the Museum to know about it because of the way he left here."

"I'm glad you decided not to lie, Mr. Murray. I was fairly certain you knew Mr. Chandler about fifteen minutes ago."

"Mr. Emerson knows?"

"He suspects. We spoke a great deal about Mr. Chandler, and in the course of the conversation it came out that he'd done postgraduate work at Harvard. So had you, and your stay had overlapped his by about two years. I thought it would have been strange if you two hadn't run into each other, especially since you were both in the same division —history of art."

"Department, yes."

"I had no definite proof one way or the other, but I probably would have found out the truth sooner or later, and then it wouldn't have been so good—for either of you."

"But you can't actually *suspect* Alan."

"We have, at the moment, no concrete evidence pointing to Mr. Chandler," Sugrue said blandly, "but on the other hand we haven't eliminated him from our thinking."

"But he's a *friend* of mine."

"Mmm," Sugrue said, and moved on to a Renoir still life.

Alan suspected of murder? It was incredible. Roger decided he'd better get in touch with him. "Can I ask you one other question?" Murray said to the lieutenant's back.

"Go right ahead."

"Well, do you think the robbery at Fischer's has anything to do with Mr. Gould's murder?"

When Sugrue turned around, Murray noticed he was wearing something like a spontaneous smile. "I'm afraid you're letting your imagination run away with you there," he said.

"You're letting your imagination run wild," was the way Ira Murray put it. "Curiosity will be the death of you, Rodge boy. I remember," he said, taking a bite of an Oreo cookie, "that when you were little you always used to wonder how people went to the bathroom on airplanes. You didn't wonder how they managed to fly, just what happened when you flushed the toilet. I believe you thought there was some magic involved."

"I also thought, since we didn't move out of Manhattan till I was ten, that pavement was the natural condition of the earth's surface, and that you had to dig down with a pickax to get at the layer of soil underneath, but I got over both of those delusions before I was eight."

"The curiosity's still there, Rodge. I think you should forget all about this murder business and buckle down to work. I'd like to see you publish a few more articles myself."

"What is this, Ira? Have you been speaking to Mother again?"

The two of them were seated at the blue lacquered kitchen table in the Ira Murrays' Seventy-ninth Street apartment. Ira's wife Martha was clearing away the dinner dishes, rinsing them off, and depositing them in the dishwasher. She was pointedly staying out of the conversation, probably a wise course since everyone knew her opinions anyway and they would only inflame Ira. Martha believed in what she called "freedom of the spirit," which meant, Roger concluded, that a person should do just what he liked provided— and it was an important "provided"—that no one suffered as a result. Especially no one from a minority group. Ira, on the other hand, believed in something called "the solid citizen." This was a concept he'd encountered in a book entitled (believe it or not) *Beyond "Beyond Good and Evil,"* and the thesis was that once every citizen was "solid," wars would be a thing of the past, slum housing would be swallowed up into the ground, bus drivers would greet passengers with a smile, somehow even disease would vanish from the face of the earth. If you gave it a little thought—as Roger had—it was thoroughly understandable that the two of them had stayed married for five years.

"Now seriously, Rodge," Ira said, "why do you have to go poking your nose into all this? I think Alan can take care of himself."

"Take care of himself? Listen, it's for my own peace of mind. *I,* at least, care about my friends."

"Inferring that I don't."

"You mean 'implying,' and if the shoe fits."

"Oh, come on. I'm very fond of Alan," Ira said, "but I don't see that there's anything here to fly off the handle about."

"A good friend of yours is about to be accused of murder and you don't see anything to fly off the handle about. Very nice."

Martha halted her cleaning operations to say, "Why don't you call him, Roger? Find out if the police have talked to him or what."

"I tried him about half an hour ago. He wasn't home. And that in itself is odd; he's always home around dinnertime."

41

"You could try him at the Museum of Fine Arts tomorrow."

"All right, honeybunch," Ira said. "I think we understand your position. Now why don't you go inside and get us the TV section so we can see what's on the tube tonight, hmm?"

Martha silently obeyed and Roger watched her walk elegantly into the living room. When she was well out of earshot he said to Ira, "What kind of a thing was that?"

"What?" Ira's head snapped around.

"Ordering her around like that. It wouldn't hurt, you know, to use the word 'please' once in a while."

"Now who's sounding like Mother?"

"I mean it, Ira. You do an awful lot of talking about this 'solid citizen' of yours. Well, I don't think *you're* very solid."

"I'm like a rock. Listen, the old girl enjoys it."

"The old girl enjoys what?" Martha said, reentering and casually tossing the newspaper down in front of Ira.

"Nothing, sweetie. Just discussing the Market." Ira made his living as a stockbroker.

"The Market is an old girl?"

"Um, I think," Roger said, "I'm going to go inside and try calling Alan again."

But there was still no answer at Alan's apartment in Cambridge, and the following day Murray's job at the Metropolitan began in earnest. Even his lunch hour was taken up in composing a letter to the National Gallery in London (the National Gallery!) requesting the loan of a painting for the forthcoming Poussin show. The question of Chandler's being accused of murder slipped Murray's mind, and even if he'd remembered, there was no time to place a call to Boston.

On Saturday morning Murray strolled over to Central Park. It was April and the sky was uncertain. There were large opaque clouds (which proved by contrast that the sky in New York is the same as it is everywhere else—blue), but they seemed undecided as to whether to blow off or to remain and marshal their forces for a shower. Walking downtown along one of the paved paths, Murray watched buxom women trying to quell the yapping of their French poodles, shabby old men lounging in solitude on the wooden benches, and bunches of hippies and near-hippies doing everything in their power to disassociate themselves from the rest of humanity. At the model-boat pond he stopped to marvel. Around the concrete shore of the pond launchings were being staged with great spontaneity. A father, more eager than his son to test the seaworthiness of the vessel, held his child's wrist untrustingly. A baby-sitter on the opposite coast back-seat-drove the whole ceremony for her charge but stoutly refused to get her fingers wet. A serious student of the sport, aged fourteen or so, guided his scale model of the *Cutty Sark* into the water with a surgeon's care, pausing only to demonstrate kingly disdain for those who viewed the endeavor lightly. Something had to be said for a city that devoted property worth millions to such pastimes.

On one of the benches near the pond Murray spotted a very pretty girl. She was wearing a wool jumper and patterned stockings and had beautiful long dark hair. She was reading and at the same time eating a box of Cracker Jacks. There had to be some way of starting a conversation with her, but how? Nice day? Trite. What's that you're reading, Hesse? It probably wasn't Hesse. (In any case, he'd never read Hesse.) What about, I haven't eaten a box of Cracker Jacks in I can't remember how long? No, not very provocative.

He walked over and took a seat next to her. "Nice day, isn't it?"

She apparently hadn't heard.

"Ahem. It's very nice out today, isn't it?"

The girl raised her head. "Were you speaking to me?"

"Yes. Oh, I liked that very much," he said, nodding at the book. "Very interesting ideas he's got."

"He?" she closed the paperback cover, and he could see that the book was *Middlemarch*. That about finished him; anyone who didn't know George Eliot was a woman couldn't be much. She let her head fall back to its previous position.

"I thought it was Hesse," Murray said lamely.

43

The girl raised her head again, this time more quickly. "Do you like Hesse? I just adore him myself."

"I like him, yes."

"Say, do you mind if I ask you a question? Do you always go around picking up girls in Central Park?"

"Only during months with an *r* in them."

She was unamused. The question had clearly been asked for sociological reasons and not out of curiosity about his personality.

"Are you reading that book for a course at some school?" Murray tried.

"No, I just read a lot, generally. Why, are you in school?"

"I'm finished. I just wrote a thesis."

"For a doctorate?" His stock was going up.

"Yes, in art history. I'm working at the Metropolitan."

"Museum?"

"That's the one."

"Oh, that's very good. Do you paint or anything?"

"No—no talent. I just do criticism."

"Is that right? I write poetry myself."

Of course she did. In addition she unquestionably had a menial job that she detested, but was holding onto it until the public became aware of her talents and started beating a path to her door. "Professionally?" he inquired.

"Oh no. Right now I'm working as a secretary. That's just so I can eat. Until I can get, you know, established. I've sent some of my work to those Little Reviews, but none of it's been published yet."

"Maybe you ought to try some Big Reviews," Murray suggested.

"Hmm?"

"Nothing. Have you ever considered teaching?"

"No," she said pensively, "I don't think I'm cut out for the academic life. I'm terrifically undisciplined."

"It's more or less universal," Murray said.

Several minutes later, he excused himself, pleading an appointment with his analyst. So, he thought on the way back to his brother's, the move to New York had changed nothing. He still talked to strange girls on the street. In Cambridge he'd done it in supermarkets near Harvard Square. Picked them up, found out their names—this one was an exception in that respect—and wrote the information down on a bookmark. Always a bookmark; he refused to keep an address book. His bookmarks overflowed with girls' names. But why?—that was the question. He rarely if ever called them or saw them again. The whole thing was futile; girls he took a serious interest in invariably were introduced to him by friends or fell into his lap some other way.

What was the point? He didn't know, but somehow he thought it had to do with the arguments Ira and Martha had been having for the last few months. He recalled that the first time he'd tried (with disastrous results) to talk to a strange girl was the day after he'd returned to Cambridge after visiting his brother several months ago and that during that visit Martha had said at one point, "God, Ira, you've been married to me for almost five years, and you still don't know the first thing about me."

By Monday the urgent need to get in touch with Alan Chandler had resprouted in Murray's mind. But he almost didn't get the chance to call him again. From ten to eleven Mr. Emerson had him scurrying to various other departments consulting with curators on gallery lighting techniques. Emerson, it seemed, had just run across a revolutionary lighting system in a trade magazine article and wanted to see what other staff members thought of it.

When Murray returned to the European paintings office at about ten after eleven he encountered a new face. Its owner was a small thin woman probably in her fifties. Her face not only had a relaxed air to it but also was the kind that induces relaxation in those who come in contact with her. "I don't think we've been introduced before," she said as Murray, somewhat out of breath, came through the door. "I'm Elizabeth Mayer." She spoke with a charming accent that would have been hard to pin down, except that Murray knew all about her already from Chandler. When she was in

45

her teens her family had fled Czechoslovakia when the Nazis had invaded. Her father had been a tailor (and an organizer) and her mother, of all things, a university professor. Sanity ran in her family, and Mrs. Mayer had inherited several generations worth of it. Unlike Thalia Reynolds she never feared breaking a rule if her conscience refused to allow her to obey it. On the other hand, she left no uncertainty about just why she was doing so. She had a blind trust in the power of logic; sudden impulses were unknown to her. Chandler had been dying to know how she'd gotten through fifty-odd years of life with an outlook like that, but of course he'd never asked her.

Murray introduced himself.

"Oh, yes," Elizabeth Mayer said. "You're the one who discovered the dead body of Mr. Gould." She looked at him as though she expected a modest denial of the feat.

Murray nodded.

"Have you spoken to your friend Mr. Chandler recently?"

"How did you find out—"

"That he was a friend of yours? Oh, I think everyone here knows about it ever since that policeman—what's his name? Mr. Stoneface—was here. I wouldn't worry about it."

"It's just because of the way Alan left here . . ."

"Oh, I understand perfectly how you feel, but you don't have a thing to be concerned about from me. You see, I was one of the very few people here who asked the Director to keep Mr. Chandler on, and not to accept his resignation."

"Alan never told me that."

"I don't believe he knew."

Murray looked very carefully at her face and then said, "Do you know anything about what happened? I mean, why or anything."

"Why he resigned? Because he didn't get promoted."

"No, I mean, why he didn't get the promotion. Alan told me he thought he was much more qualified than Mr. Gould. That is—"

"Oh, I can believe that. But he was young, he was inexperienced," she said wistfully. "Mr. Chandler, I'm talking

46

about. Mr. Gould could hardly have been called either young *or* inexperienced. In any case I don't know all the details. Why don't you ask Miss Reynolds or Mr. Emerson. I think they'd know more than I do."

Murray decided he might just do that. "Actually I was about to call Alan in Boston. I've tried to get him at home but he doesn't answer. I thought I'd try the museum where he works."

"Well, don't let me keep you, Mr. Murray. Very nice to have met you," and she was off down the long branch of the L of offices.

Murray entered Mr. Emerson's office and found it empty. Then he recalled that the curator had said something about leaving for lunch a little early. He picked up the receiver of the telephone on Emerson's desk and told the operator he wanted to call the Boston Museum of Fine Arts. She didn't think to ask whether or not it was personal business, as she usually did.

"Museum of Fine Arts," said a snappy female voice at the other end a short time later.

"I'd like to speak to Alan Chandler, please."

"One moment, pl—" She cut herself off and rang another phone.

"Library, Miss Warshaw," said a voice after three and a half rings.

Library? That didn't seem likely, but Murray nevertheless said, "I'd like to speak to Alan Chandler, please," for the second time.

"Mr. Hamlin isn't in right now, could I take a message?"

"No, listen, I don't want Mr. Hamlin. I'm looking for Alan Chandler. Chandler—C-H-A—"

"Oh, you've got the wrong extension. This is the library. He's not in this department at all. Hang on. I'll try to get the operator back again."

After several pumps of the receiver button the snappy voice from before came back on the line. "Opratuh."

"Operator, this gentleman doesn't want Mr. Hamlin. He's trying to get Mr. *Chandler*."

"Oh, just one mo—" She cut herself off again and there were some more rings, this time unanswered.

"Operator," Murray said, in the unlikely event she'd remained on the wire. "*Operator*." Oh God, he was losing his mind. Now he had the idea that if he screamed loud enough the sound of his voice might penetrate a closed line.

But the snappy voice finally returned. "Did you get your party?" she asked, pronouncing the last word like a diminutive of Patricia, in true Boston fashion.

"No, I didn't, and—"

"Wait a second, I'll try another department."

She was as good as her word. In another several seconds a voice said, "Conservation, King here."

Murray wondered briefly if the conservation department up there was governed by a monarchy and then said, "I'd like to speak to Alan Chandler."

"I'm afraid he's not in this department. His extension is—"

"I think the operator's already tried his extension, though I wouldn't swear to it. He doesn't answer. You wouldn't have any idea where I could reach him."

"Not me, but you might try Mr. Hallowell. He's also in paintings. I'll see if I can get the switchboard again."

With the hand that wasn't holding the receiver Murray wiped off some sweat that had mysteriously collected on his forehead.

"Opratuh."

"Operator, this man would like to find out where Mr. Chandler is. Would you ring Mr. Hallowell for him, that's 539."

"Ringing 539," said the operator.

"And, please, this is long distance," Murray reminded her, but the last three words were heard only by the circuit. He rolled his eyes around several times in their sockets and switched the receiver to the other ear.

"Mr. Hallowell's office." This was undoubtedly a secretary.

"Could I speak to Mr. Hallowell, please."

"Who is this calling?"

48

"He won't know me. But I'm calling from the Metropolitan Museum in New York."

"Hallowell," said a male voice almost instantaneously. "Can I help you?"

"God, I hope so. I'm trying to get ahold of Alan Chandler. A man I was just talking to, Mr. King, I believe, said you might know where he is."

"Oh, yes, King, in Conservation, fine fellow. But I'm afraid Mr. Chandler's not in today. Hasn't been in for the last few days, in fact. Phoned last Thursday, I think it was, to say he caught the flu. Doctor ordered him to stay in bed for a while."

"In bed? But that's impos—" Murray caught himself up. There was no sense losing Alan a second museum job in one year.

"I beg your pardon."

"I was going to say, it's very unlike Alan to be sick. He doesn't catch things easily."

"Oh, right you are, strong as an ox, but this time, apparently, the bug got him. Too bad. Is it anything I can help you with?"

"No, it's a, um, personal matter."

"In that case, why don't you call back in a few days. I'm sure he'll be back by then. You know how these bugs are: hang around for a few days, then poof! they're gone."

"I'll do that. Thank you." He hung up.

So Alan had lied to the Museum of Fine Arts. Alan Chandler! Lying! Something damn important must have come up. What in God's name could have happened to him? Had he been scared of the police? Murray couldn't figure it out, but it certainly seemed that, to paraphrase Mr. Hallowell, poof! *he* was gone.

FOUR

By WEDNESDAY OF THAT WEEK Murray had made several more attempts to get in touch with Chandler, both at his home and at the Museum of Fine Arts, but he'd had no luck. On that day, however, a new source of excitement arrived: the auction of the Cézanne. It was to be held that evening at Fischer's auction rooms, and during the day an underground current of anticipation ran through the European paintings department. But it remained underground; like a no-hitter, it was apparently bad form to discuss the sale of the picture before it was consummated.

Late in the afternoon Murray could no longer contain himself. Unbound by tradition, he asked Mr. Emerson, "Who's going to represent the Museum tonight at Fischer's?"

Emerson's face sagged. "I'm afraid I'm the lucky one."

Mr. Ferris, who had been a little less able to bottle up his emotions than the rest of the department, interrupted his chat with Sandy Janis to remark, "Don't let him fool you, Roger. He's just pretending. I happen to know he put in a special request to the Director asking to represent us tonight."

50

Eyes turned to Emerson.

"I just wanted to create as little disturbance about this thing as possible. If someone else went we'd have a circus."

"Well, congratulations," Murray said.

"No call for that," Emerson said. "I must say you seem very wrought up about the whole thing."

"You have to admit it isn't every day we get a chance to bid on a million-dollar painting. I'd give anything to be there myself."

"Would you? It's not quite in the league with the gunfight at the OK Corral as far as excitement goes. Haven't you ever been to an auction?"

"Once. The chief item of the day was an antique duck decoy."

Emerson's eyes seemed to twinkle as they studied Murray, and his lips came as close as they ever came to forming a smile. "Why don't you come along, then?" he offered indifferently. "I don't think there'd be any insuperable objections."

"Do you think I could?"

"Why not? I'll let the people know over at Fischer's. All you have to do is tell the man at the door you're with me. I *think* that should be sufficient to get you in."

For the rest of the day Murray walked around in a nervous high. Chandler was forgotten. So was more trivial Museum business. Even the article Sandy brought to his attention just before closing time didn't arouse the laughter it might have otherwise. The article was on the third page of the *Daily News,* a paper that turned up infrequently around the European paintings office, and added little to the general knowledge. But the headline was being passed around with gusto: COPS SCAN MUSEUM MAN MURDER PIX it read.

Murray practically danced back to his brother's at five. When dinner was over he retired to the bathroom, and when he came out he had on his best suit, a pinstriped, wide-lapel number. Brushing off a few stray oohs and aahs from Ira and Martha, he left for Fischer's.

In the lobby of Fischer's building a uniformed guard from

a private security agency was taking credentials. Most of the guests merely flashed their invitations and were waved through, but Murray had none and was held up. It took a call to Fischer himself on the house telephone to clinch the matter finally in his favor.

Upstairs a large number of men in business suits and a few in black tie milled about. There were several women too but they appeared to be doing everything they could to become invisible. The noise level was that of a very subdued dinner party as heard from the other side of a soundproof wall. Every now and then a voice was raised to say something like, "Well, the last time *I* was at the Tate . . ." or "Yes, but you know his wife wants to sell the entire collection, lock, stock, and barrel." The auction room itself, which adjoined one of the exhibition rooms, was gradually filling. It was a large auditorium-like room with long rows of wooden folding chairs. Some of the bidders had already taken their seats, and except for the surroundings they might have been waiting for the dentist to be free so he could examine them. At the rear of the rows of chairs were two large tapestries that made part of the room into an entrance hall. The tapestries, like everything else, were extremely worn.

Murray entered the auction room and immediately spotted Emerson talking to some people who were sitting in the first row. When Emerson raised his eyes from them for a second Murray signaled and the curator immediately excused himself and headed back toward the rear of the room. "I see you made it," he said to Murray.

"Yes, I wanted to thank—"

Emerson waved his hands. "Have you seen the picture?"

"Uh, no. You see, the afternoon you sent me over here—"

"Then you must take a look at it. Mr. Fischer!" He twirled an index finger in the air, and in another few seconds the gallery owner emerged from the interior of a small group of men down the aisle. "Mr. Fischer, I believe you already know our Mr. Murray here, the new curatorial assistant."

Fischer nodded, then he turned to Emerson. "I'm sorry, I have a great many people to see—"

"Oh, I think you could spare a moment to let Mr. Murray see the famous Cézanne."

"Now?"

"Why not? The poor boy's dying to get a look at it."

Fischer scowled, pulled at his chin, and said, "Come with me." On the way out he turned back to give Emerson another dirty look.

While Murray wondered if Mr. Emerson had been drinking (or perhaps had just received a refund from the Internal Revenue) Fischer led him into a back hallway with several wooden-paneled doorways on either wall. The dealer went straight to one of the doors and opened it with a key from his pocket, revealing a room even more seedy than any of the public galleries. The oriental rug on the floor had hardly any color at all left in it, and the walls were unbelievably dirty. In the center of one windowless wall a large oil painting was propped up on a velvet-upholstered display stand.

It was a breathtaking work, clearly one of the finest examples of Cézanne's art. All of the artist's recurrent themes were present; the battle between two- and three-dimensionality was intense. Yet the subject itself was simple: a wooden bridge across a narrow river with a mountain, no doubt Mont St. Victoire, in the background. The bridge itself interested Murray especially. The painting, like so many other Cézannes, looked unfinished, and in some passages the painting of the bridge melted into the drawing of the preliminary sketch and even into bare canvas. Murray stood motionless in front of the picture.

" 'Le Pont des Trois Sautets,' " Fischer announced in his broken French. "You like?"

"It's . . . magnificent . . ."

"Wait a minute, quiet a minute. Did you hear someone call me? I thought I heard—"

He was right. From the auction room a voice was saying, "Mr. Fischer, could you come here a moment? Mr. Fischer? Mr. *Fischer*."

"Coming, coming," he called back. To Murray he said, "You just stay here a minute, okay, and keep your eye on the painting. I don't want you to leave this spot, okay?" And he scurried out the door saying, "Coming, coming, I've only got two legs, for heaven's sake."

Murray watched the empty doorway for a time, then turned back to the picture. He'd inched up to it in order to get a closer look at the brushwork when he sensed someone outside the door of the room. There was a quiet shuffling in the hallway, and a face poked itself in through the doorway. Just a face; at first it seemed that there was no body attached. The face was lined and leathery, and its eyes blinked continually. For several seconds Murray could only stare rudely. Then the face began to edge around the door in a rubbery manner, somehow evoking in Murray the image of a cartoon character peeking out from behind a tree that was considerably narrower than his body. Two arms next emerged into the light of the room, and in the hand at the end of one was a mop. Finally, the owner of these parts was entirely inside the room, and Murray noticed that although his posture was atrocious he possessed surprisingly broad shoulders.

The man's first acknowledgment of Murray's presence was a sheepish smile. Thereafter, he addressed all remarks to his mop. "Don't let me bother you none," he said. "You just go right on doing whatever you're doing. I'm just the clean-up man."

Uncertain as to whether or not this constituted a formal introduction, Murray kept still and continued studying the painting.

"Yup, you go right ahead. I won't be in your way." He started making some guttural noises which Murray realized were his equivalent of humming.

"You're not disturbing me. I was just taking a look at this painting that's going up for sale tonight."

"Just the clean-up man cleaning up," he said. "Sometimes work during the day, sometimes at night. Cleaning up, you know."

"That's fine with me."

"Fine with me," he echoed moronically. "Yup, just go

around sweeping and mopping, mopping and sweeping. Sometimes I find things, sometimes I don't."

"Yuh, well, I suppose I ought to be going back into the other room now. Don't want to miss the auction."

The janitor was blocking the doorway, however, and was showing no signs of getting ready to move. "Got something here might interest you, maybe," he said, still apparently speaking to the mop.

Murray wondered for a second or two if the man was about to fix it up with a nice female mop, then he remembered Fischer's request that he remain with the painting—perhaps the gallery owner had had this very contingency in mind—and he decided he might as well hear the man out. "Something that might interest me?"

"Might, and then again it might not." He reached around the door of the room, which was still ajar, and brought in a plastic pail filled with sloshing soapy water.

Murray acknowledged the pail. "Actually," he said, "I'm not really in the market for a pail just now, but thanks anyway."

"Pail?" The man was thoroughly bewildered.

"You said you had something that might interest me. But I'm afraid I don't have much call for a pail right at the moment and—"

"Oh-ooh. Ooh, I see, you thought I meant the pail," and he went into a sort of asthmatic laughter. "No, that's not what I had in mind. Not at all." He laughed a little more. "Use that to clean the floor, you see."

Murray sighed pointedly.

"Now what I thought you might be interested in's right here in my pocket." He shoved a hand into his Levi's, rummaged around a bit, straight-armed, and pulled out a closed fist. Then he held out his arm as if he was going to ask for guesses on the fist's contents.

Murray dutifully came over to take a look. The man opened his hand and disclosed (in addition to an intricately lined palm) a yellow square of cardboard with a large red numeral, 57403, across the top edge, and underneath that the words *Universal Security Loan Co.*

"A pawn ticket," said Murray, who knew of the existence of such things only through O. Henry stories.

"That's what it is, all right," said the janitor. "I found it on the floor last Tuesday morning, you see."

"That's very nice, but I think you should return it to Mr. Fischer."

"Oh, it's nothing belonging to him. I asked him. No, no, he don't have any business with pawn tickets."

"But someone visiting the gallery probably lost it. They might come back looking for it."

The man chose merely to smile in response to this. "Now what I had in mind, you see, was this. I thought maybe someone—someone a little more respectable than me, I'm just a clean-up man—someone might just go down and redemption it for me."

Murray's face was blank.

"And of course, that someone'd be entitled to half of whatever it was pawned."

The light dawned. "You want me—Oh, no, I couldn't do that. I mean, I think you should return it."

"Aw, nobody's missing it."

"Besides, I don't think you understand how these things work. You see, I'd have to *pay* to get whatever it was that was—Wait a minute. Did you say last Tuesday?"

"Huh?" Total bewilderment again.

"When did you say you found this? Did you say last Tuesday?"

"In the morning, right. I remember 'cause Charley and me had a little bit of a binge the night before. Charley's my buddy and he's getting married, so we gave him a little party, you see. Fifty-three Charley is but spry as a—"

"But that was the morning after the robbery."

"Yeah, come to think of it, I did hear something about somebody breaking in here the night before. Wouldn't know much about that, though."

"But this might be evidence. It might have been dropped

by the people who broke in. You should turn it over to the police."

"Police! Oh, no, not me. Listen here, I don't mess with the police, they don't mess with me. And I like it fine just that way." He shook his head. Then after a time he said, "Maybe, I just better hold onto this thing myself. Find somebody else to go redemption it. Charley, maybe."

Murray cleared his throat. "Um, I think we could work something out. I think you had a good idea there. I could go down there myself and—"

"No, no, wouldn't want you to go to any trouble. I think I can get it all straightened out."

"Listen, I could promise not to bring the police in." Murray bit his lip. "I could just redeem the ticket, and no one would have to know. We could split whatever it was."

"I don't know. Maybe—"

"No police, no trouble, nothing. I can be very discreet."

"All right." The janitor grudgingly handed over the ticket. "You'll let me know soon as you go down to that store now."

"Absolutely."

There was a slight commotion outside the door, and Fischer reentered. "What's going on in here? Mr. Emerson's having conniptions out there. He thinks I kidnaped you."

"You told me to stay right here," Murray said.

"Did I? And you, Ziwicki. I thought I gave strict orders you should never come in this room."

Ziwicki, the clean-up man, apologized unintelligibly and left.

"Never understands a thing I tell him," Fischer said to Murray, hustling him out the door and back down the corridor to the auction room. "Not too much up here, you know what I mean?" When they arrived he said, "Mr. Emerson's around here somewhere. You find him. I've still got a thousand people to see," and he went off mumbling, "Never understands a thing, that guy. Not a damn thing . . ."

Emerson was sitting on an aisle seat in the fifth row of folding chairs and was reserving the seat next to his. Most of the low-key discussion groups that had been scattered around the hall when Murray left were now disbanded, and there was a general movement of settling down throughout the room. Murray sidestroked his way to the chair Emerson was saving for him and sat down.

"Well," Emerson said, "what did you think? Should we plunk down our three dollars and ninety-eight cents or not?"

"You don't really want us to get this picture, do you?" Murray was serious.

"I don't mind the picture. It's the publicity I don't like."

"But we can't—"

"I know, you want great art, you have to pay, and money is what brings 'em in. I've heard that from Ferris and the rest of them till it's coming out my ears. But the whole thing's like a circus. You know there's another roomful of people upstairs watching on closed-circuit TV?"

Up on the small ramshackle stage at the front of the room several men were moving about. All but one had on work uniforms. The non-uniformed man was in a gray suit and was making his way to the lectern in the center of the stage. He was a square-jawed, Clark Kent sort with horn-rimmed glasses, and he carried a soft leather zippered case under one arm.

"Is that the auctioneer?" Murray asked, nodding at the man.

"Leach," Emerson said, "one of the best in the business. There's a rumor he once ran up the price of an ashtray from the Statler Hilton to seventeen dollars and fifty cents."

Up front Leach picked up a wooden gavel from the rostrum and banged it once, not vehemently but with authority. Gradually, the last remaining standees filtered to their seats; the clanking and scraping of folding chairs died down.

Leach surveyed the crowd. "All right there, if everyone is seated I think we can begin. You gentlemen at the rear, there are two vacant seats on the side over there." His voice was being transmitted through a public-address system that seemed designed to decrease volume rather than increase it. The words had a pinched quality, as if they were coming from miles away. He adjusted his glasses and said, "First on

58

my list tonight is the 'Reclining Woman,' by Matisse, that's number 32574 in the catalogue, you can take a look at it right over there if you wish." He pointed to another velvet display stand, larger than the one Murray had seen in the back room, on which two attendants were positioning the painting. "All right there, that's number 32574." His voice was entirely without inflection; he might have been talking about yesterday's weather.

Along the front of the room spotters had taken up positions and were sizing up the crowd. "Well, now," Leach said, "I'd like to start the bidding at ten thousand. Do I hear ten thousand? Ten thousand? Do I hear ten thousand? Ten thousand I have ten thousand, ten thousand five do I see ten five, ten, ten five, ten, ten five, I have ten five, ten five, eleven, ten five, eleven, eleven, I have eleven, will someone say eleven five? I have eleven five in two places . . ."

It was all going forward at a dizzying clip. Leach's words chugged out with the effortless efficiency of a Rolls-Royce engine. He would look at the painting, glance at the audience, check his spotters, and glance back at the audience. Meanwhile, there was dead silence from among the folding chairs.

Murray leaned over and whispered to Emerson, "How does he do it?"

"Do what?"

"Know where all the bids are coming from."

"There are signals," Emerson said. "Each one has his own and Leach knows them all. He probably doesn't even use the spotters. The man's a virtuoso."

"But why? Why do they need signals?"

"Murray," Emerson said sternly, "these are people representing some of the richest art collectors and most important museums in the world. You don't expect them to shout when they want attention, do you?"

". . . fourteen thousand, fourteen, fourteen five, will someone say fourteen five? do I hear fourteen five? ladies and gentlemen, this painting is worth much more than that, I have fourteen five . . ."

"Have we been doing any of the bidding?" Murray whispered.

"No, he knows the items the Met's bidding on already. We have a standing bid. I don't even have to do anything except keep my pencil on my knee like this, eraser down." He demonstrated.

"No kidding. Do you think I could scratch my nose without it being interpreted as a bid?"

". . . I have eighteen five once . . . Eighteen thousand five hundred dollars twice . . . Done! That's number, uh, seventeen, I believe?" He looked out over the heads to the right-hand part of one of the rear rows. "Number seventeen is correct." One of the attendants noted down the information on a clipboard. "Now," Leach said, "number two on my list tonight is . . ."

Emerson shook his head. "Not worth half that," he said. "Three years ago you could have had that Matisse for six, maybe six five."

Several more paintings were knocked down at prices Emerson thought excessive before the time came for the Cézanne. It was larger than any of the other paintings so far and plainly more important. The attendants seemed to take extra care getting it on the display stand. Leach stared sidelong at it for about ten seconds before he said anything. But when he finally did, his tone of voice was the same as before. "We now come to number 32653 in the catalogue, a landscape by, um, Cézanne. 'Les Pont des Trois Sautets,' the bridge of the three Sautets. Some of you know that this painting was formerly in the collection of the late James Aldeburg." He shuffled some papers into order on the rostrum. "Well, then. I would like to start the bidding at seven hundred thousand dollars. And could we please proceed in jumps of fifty thousand, I think, on this one. *If* that is agreeable to everyone, hmm?" He made a thin smile and scanned the audience.

Emerson gave Murray a meaningful look.

"All right then, ladies and gentlemen, I have six hundred thousand, do I hear seven hundred thousand? seven hundred thousand, I have seven hundred thousand, seven, seven fifty, seven, seven fifty, seven fifty! seven fifty is bid, seven fifty, eight, seven fifty, eight, eight, eight, I have eight, eight, eight fifty, eight, eight fifty . . ."

Emerson's pencil was standing upright on his knee, held in the middle by a thumb and forefinger.

"How high are we prepared to go?" Murray asked.

"One, five," Emerson answered brusquely.

"One mil—!"

"Shh."

Most of the people in the folding chairs were now extending their chins as if they were having difficulty seeing over the heads in front of them. If Murray observed closely he could catch a small motion by an onlooker that was probably a bid. Although, as with the third-base coach on a baseball diamond, it was difficult to tell which chin scratchings were significant and which were merely to relieve an itch.

". . . Nine, nine fifty, nine, nine fifty, nine fifty! I see nine fifty, will anyone say one million, one million, one million, do I have one million? one million! one million dollars is the bid . . ."

Emerson's pencil was still poised in a straight vertical position, and Murray was watching it as if it were about to perform a difficult gymnastic feat of its own accord.

"There's someone on the other side of the room," Emerson announced in a whisper, "who's also very anxious to get their hands on this picture."

"How do you know?"

"Bidding's moving very fast. You see how Leach always looks over that way and then over here to see if the pencil's still up?"

"Who is it?"

"Haven't the foggiest. Probably one of those big boys from Houston or Dallas."

". . . one million three, I have one million three, one million three, will anyone make it one million three fifty, one million three fifty, do I see one million three fifty, ladies and gentlemen this painting is practically priceless, one million three fifty! . . ."

"One million three seventy-five," piped up a creaky voice somewhere near the back of the room, and heads swiveled.

Leach halted his patter. "I'm sorry, sir," he said in a tone subtly colored by a great many emotions, none of which, however, was regret, "but the bidding must proceed by fifty thousand. Do I hear one million four? If not, of course . . . Ah, one million four hundred thousand, I have one million four, one four, one four, one four fifty, one four, one four fifty, do I see one four fifty? . . ." And he was off again.

"It's getting pretty close now," Murray whispered.

Emerson was gazing straight ahead.

". . . one million five, do I see one five, one five, one five, I have one million five hundred thousand! . . ." The pace was slowing.

"Is that us?" Murray said.

Emerson gave a slight, but forbidding, nod.

"One million five hundred thousand dollars is bid. Do I hear one million five fifty? I have one and a half, will anyone make it one million five fifty?" Leach turned to his spotters. After a second or two he said, "I have one million five hundred and fifty thousand dollars!"

Murray looked over at Emerson. Gradually, forlornly, the pencil came down, and Emerson almost imperceptibly shook his head. Murray felt a great urge to cry out. What he could say he didn't quite know, but there was a terrific impulse to say something.

But Leach was speaking again. "Wait a minute, wait a minute, ladies and gentlemen. My attendant now informs me there was no bid of one million five hundred and fifty thousand. Therefore, the last bid of one million five hundred thousand till stands. I hope you will accept my sincere apologies on behalf of my attendant over here"—he looked over to his left—"and I trust"—long pause—"it will not happen again." He shuffled the papers on the rostrum. "Now. The high bid is one million five hundred thousand dollars.

Do I hear one million five fifty?" Leach looked around the room.

Emerson turned to Murray and said, "I believe that man would wrap the painting with his own mother's flesh if he thought it would up the price."

"You mean, all that stuff about his spotter making a mistake—"

"Flimflam, nothing but flimflam. And it almost worked."

"Last call," Leach was saying. "I have one million five hundred thousand dollars . . . once . . . twice . . ." Bang! went the gavel. "Done!" said Leach.

Scattered applause broke out.

Emerson slumped back in his chair as if he'd just completed three sets of tennis. "Well," he said, "the Metropolitan Museum has another spectacle on its hands."

FIVE

THURSDAY NIGHT, the evening following the auction, Murray tried calling Alan Chandler's Cambridge apartment once more. This time, after three rings, the phone was picked up.

"Hello."

"Alan, is that you? What the hell happened to you? Where have you been hiding?"

"I'm sorry," said the voice at the other end, now clearly not Chandler's. "Alan Chandler doesn't live here anymore."

Roger was silent a moment. Then he said, "What do you mean, doesn't live here anymore?"

"I don't see how I can make it any plainer. He's moved out. He's gone. He doesn't come home here every night. In fact, he doesn't come here at all."

"Do you know where he moved to?"

"He didn't leave a forwarding address. I only saw him once, for a few minutes, to sign a sublet agreement."

"Is there anyone there who might know where he went? I'm very anxious to get in touch with him."

"So am I," said the new occupant of the apartment meaningly. "And so is the telephone company. He didn't pay his last bill, and they're being very unpleasant about it. So if you find him I'd appreciate it if you'd ask him to get me off the hook and pay his goddamn bill."

"I'll do that," Murray said blankly, but the line was already dead.

Incredible! Chandler had vanished into thin air. He'd called in sick at the Museum, rented his apartment, and flown the coop. The question was, where had he flown *to*?

Roger went into the living room and delivered the news to Ira and Martha. Martha frowned and dropped a stitch in her knitting, something she did very infrequently. Ira put down the *New York Times* (which he held it his civic duty to read front page to last every day, and which, therefore, he had to cart home with him from work) and said, "This whole thing is ridiculous, Rodge. Alan's moved to another apartment and forgot to leave a forwarding address. He probably needed a couple of days to get his belongings into his new place, so he told the Museum up there he was sick."

"Alan, lie?"

"Who is he, George Washington, he can't lie?"

"He could have moved his stuff into a new apartment over a weekend. It couldn't have taken this long."

"If it'll make you feel any better I'll call a couple of people I know in Boston and ask them what happened to him," Ira offered.

"You'd do that for me?"

"Look, Rodge, sarcasm I can do without. You want me to call or don't you?"

"I want you to call."

But three calls produced no information as to Chandler's whereabouts. Ira then became even more magnanimous and volunteered to try some friends in New York, purely for his brother's peace of mind. But again there was no word of Chandler.

Where the hell had he got to?

At approximately eleven o'clock the next morning the

question was answered. Emerson, having spent a particularly exasperating morning so far, noticed once again the carton of Chandler's effects he'd asked Sandy to remove on Murray's first day at the Museum. She still hadn't gotten around to it, and when Emerson saw the box under the same table where it had been that day he blew up. "Goddamnit! Can't they do anything? What are we paying them for?" He calmed himself. "Murray, could you get that thing out of here?" he asked with more composure. "I don't like to ask you, but it's the only way it's going to get done."

"But where—I'll take care of it," Murray said.

"Thank you."

Murray silently shouldered the cardboard box and walked out into the reception room. Sandy and Doris were both at their typewriters, but the machines were silent. Thalia Reynolds was standing in front of the secretaries' desks and holding forth about a special-delivery package she was expecting in the mail. "Now I want it treated with the utmost care," she was saying. "And bring it straight to my office the moment it comes in." Then she spied Murray and the carton. "Just a minute there, young man. Where are you taking that?"

"I really don't know. Mr. Emerson just told me to put it somewhere else."

"So long as it stays out of *my* office you can put it wherever you like."

"I'll find someplace for it," Murray said dejectedly, and started off again.

"Wait a sec," Sandy said. "Why don't you try one of the storerooms? Where they keep paintings that aren't on exhibit. It should be all right there. One of the custodians can let you in."

"Thanks," Murray said, "I will." He began walking out of the reception room again. As he reached the outer door a paper flew off the top of the pile of articles in the carton. Murray stooped to retrieve it, and as he did so he noticed some of the writing on it. The paper was evidently a carbon of the letter Chandler had sent to the Museum accepting the position they'd offered him about a year ago. But the part that caught Murray's eye was the return address:

23 Jackson Farms Rd.
North Conway, New Hampshire.

At the end of the body of the letter Chandler had written, ". . . and if for any reason you should want to get in touch with me during the next two weeks I will be at the above address."

"What's that you've got there?" Thalia Reynolds asked.

"Nothing," Murray said, and departed hastily.

On the way to the storeroom he collated the information from the letter with some he'd received earlier from Chandler. Originally, the Chandlers had been from New England. They'd filtered down from Maine, stopping along the way to acquire what was at the time worthless property, mostly in New Hampshire, to convert it into usable farmland. The Chandlers were a stubborn lot, and a few of them still inhabited the ancestral homes. One of them, a great-aunt, lived in an old farmhouse in North Conway, New Hampshire. Owing largely to the death of her husband, a sizable accumulation of debts, and the ski trade, she'd been compelled to abandon the raising of crops and turn the farmhouse into a guesthouse. She'd hung on, though, to the very last, and was finally swayed only by the suggestion that she call the place after her late husband; visitors could then carry his name—but what the hell *was* his name?—back to New York and Boston and the other great centers of civilization.

And whenever he had a couple of weeks free Chandler stayed up there with old Aunt Mel—Melisande was her full given name. So that was where he was hiding out!

Murray's sense of triumph, however, lasted not even as far as the storeroom. If Chandler was really up in New Hampshire, how would Murray get in touch with him? He'd forgotten the husband's last name—it was Chandler's mother's side of the family—as well as his first, which was in the title of the hotel. It was some old-fashioned thing like Orville or

Ezekiel, but those weren't right. So how could he possibly get the phone number?

"You could always drive up there," Martha suggested that evening.

Ira, who had his soup spoon poised halfway between bowl and mouth, dropped the spoon, causing a miniature split-pea geyser. "What? Are you crazy? Drive all the way up to Conway, New Hampshire, on the off chance Alan'll be there? It's lunacy."

"*North* Conway," Roger corrected.

"I'm sorry I suggested it," Martha said.

"Well, it's sheer madness," Ira said. "Just . . . just madness."

"Everything I say is madness. Look, I said I'm sorry I brought up the idea." She moved her spoon around in the soup bowl.

"You don't have to be sorry, honeybunch. It's just that you don't give these things enough thought beforehand. Reason"—he pointed to his head—"that's what you have to use."

Roger squirmed in his chair. "Oh, come on, Ira," he said. "So what if she doesn't think out everything down to the last detail; women are *supposed* to be like that." He turned to Martha. "But I have the feeling Ira's right"—a glance back at his brother—"for once."

"Well, I don't see anything especially nutty in the idea," Martha said, and when Ira began to arrange his features into a look of horror she continued, "I was speaking to Roger, Ira. I mean, you could drive up to North Conway in five hours tomorrow and drive back on Sunday."

"It's an interesting thought," Roger said, "but entirely out of the realm of possibility."

Completely out of the question, he repeated to himself later, trying to fall asleep on the living room couch. The luminous dial of the traveling alarm clock he stood on the coffee table every night before going to bed said twelve-fifteen. He sat up and set the alarm for six-thirty.

By seven-fifteen the next morning he was turning the key in the ignition of his Tempest. Murray had driven the car down from Cambridge two weeks ago, but since then he'd gotten into it only to comply with the alternate-side-of-the-street parking regulations. That he should sell the thing as quickly as possible was one of the few opinions held jointly by Ira and Martha.

Taking with him only a small airline bag containing a change of underwear, a clean shirt and socks, and toilet articles, he pulled out of the parking space and headed for the Triborough Bridge. It was a foggy morning. The streetlights, which were still on when he set out, made starlike patterns on the windshield, and it was hard to keep the glass from clouding. On Bruckner Boulevard cars had their parking lights on. By the Connecticut Turnpike most of them had shifted over to their headlights. But a short time after he crossed the New Hampshire–Massachusetts border the sky abruptly cleared, and the day became brilliantly sunny.

The turnoff for Jackson Farms Road, Roger recalled from a previous trip, was in the center of the town of North Conway. The village, on the fringe of the White Mountains, has only a single main street, but if you look north down it on a clear day you get an imposing view of Mount Washington. On the west side of the street is an ornate, and obsolete, Victorian railroad station, the chief attraction for photographers who pass through, and a natural conversation starter. Today, with the bright sun on its roof, it looked even more obsolete than usual.

Navigating by ear, Murray found Aunt Mel's farmhouse-turned-hotel without difficulty. He ignored a sign that said THIS SPACE RESERVED FOR THE OCCUPANTS OF BERTRAM'S GUEST-HOUSE—Uncle Bertram! of course—and pulled into the small gravel lot next to the building. He left the car, leaped up onto the wooden porch, which was crowded with lawn furniture of the kind ordinarily found only in photographs of the Yalta Conference, and rang the bell.

Aunt Mel took her time coming to the door. She finally made it, though, and warily said, "Yes?" through the screen door. She had a bemused smile on her face, which Murray recalled was her natural expression. It was a look that could be very easily adapted to pity, incredulity, satisfaction, even annoyance. It was the look of a person who has never known subway rush hours or office duplicating machines. "What can I do for you, young man?"

"You don't remember me," Murray said. "But I remember you. You're Aunt Mel."

"Oh, you must be a friend of Alan's."

"Roger, Roger Murray. Don't you remember? I was here with Alan once last summer. I stayed for the weekend."

"Roger . . ." She closed her eyes and tugged at her Adam's apple.

"Murray." He looked at her expectantly.

"I don't recall any Murray, but then my memory's not what it used to be."

"Roger Murray. Murray's my last name; people are always getting confused."

"You're welcome to come in, Roger," she said. "I've got a kettle of water for tea on in the kitchen. Alan's not here, though."

Murray's face dropped. "He's not?"

"He went into town about half an hour ago. Should be back pretty soon now."

"You mean he is here!"

The smile altered slightly. "Didn't I just say he wasn't here? I don't think you listen very good, young man. Ought to have that looked into."

"I meant, he's here in New Hampshire."

"I reckon so, unless he's suddenly taken it into his head to fly away to Canada. Come on in, have some tea."

Murray walked through a hallway lined with apricot wall-paper that had a design of coaches and manor houses on it, and past a door with a sign that read LAVATORY. Aunt Mel seated him in the living room and brought him tea. Then she left him alone. He picked up a copy of *Boy's Life* magazine and began to thumb through it.

Alan appeared in the living room archway ten minutes

later. He was wearing a sweatshirt that had once belonged to the Harvard Athletic Association and was lettered "Property of H. A. A." "Roger!" he burst out. "What in the name of God are you doing here?"

Murray rose and extended his hand. "I've been calling you for a week and a half. Maybe I should be asking you that question."

"It's a long story, Rodge." He nodded toward the kitchen and said, "Maybe we ought to talk outside."

They took seats in two of the angular, wood-lath chairs on the porch. "Go ahead," Roger said when they were settled.

"Well," Chandler began, "I was on my way to work a week ago last Wednesday. Like I always do, I bought a paper at the newsstand on the island in the middle of Harvard Square, and there at the bottom of the page is this article headed, 'Metropolitan Museum Curator Found Dead in Apartment.' Of course I read it on the spot—and promptly panicked."

"Why? You were up in Boston the whole day. How could they even remotely connect you with it?"

"That's just it. I wasn't in Boston the whole day. I'd taken the day off from the Fine Arts."

"What! But why? Where'd you go?"

Chandler avoided Murray's eyes and said evenly, "To New York, as a matter of fact."

"What the hell were you doing in New York!"

"Now just take it easy, Rodge," Chandler said. "Don't get yourself into a state."

"All right, I'm taking it easy. Now will you please tell me what you were doing in New York."

Chandler looked down at his sweatshirt, noticed a spot on it, and absently tried to erase the spot with his thumb. "Well," he said, still not looking Roger in the eye, "I had to go pick up my stuff at the Museum sooner or later anyway, and . . . well, there was this girl . . ."

"Oh." The girl explained everything. Murray had never understood Alan's attitude toward girls, but at least, by now, he was no longer surprised by the symptoms. Chandler could see a girl for weeks in the course of his normal everyday routine before he might summon up the courage to speak a word to her. Having spoken to her casually for ten minutes or so, he would follow her off to Montana, if she was headed that way, in order to get better acquainted. (He'd actually followed one as far as Iowa once and dropped in on her there at her parents' farm.) He somehow found it impossible to get to know a girl in his natural surroundings. And he was so damned outspoken in other situations!

"Yes," Murray remarked, as offhandedly as he could, "Mr. Emerson's been complaining about the carton of books and things you left there." He paused. "But this girl—she must have seen you. She must have been with you at the time of the murder."

"She wasn't there," Chandler said desolately.

"What do you mean she wasn't there?"

"She didn't stop in New York apparently. I thought she was going home to visit her parents—she was in graduate school, and her family lived on the East Side of Manhattan—but she wasn't. She went down to Philadelphia to visit a friend for spring vacation."

"Didn't you even tell her you were coming? You went all the way to New York without . . ." Murray trailed off. "Well, you went to the parents' apartment, right? *They* must have seen you, at least."

"They weren't home. I called later and they told me she'd gone to Philadelphia."

Murray said nothing for a time. "But what are you afraid of?" he said finally. "You were doing something legitimate. You could have told the police just what you told me."

Chandler took time to arrange his thoughts. "If you didn't know me, Rodge, if you didn't know me very well, would you believe a story like that?"

"Of course I would."

Chandler gave an exasperated nod.

"I would, Alan."

"And there was another thing. There was all my stuff down in New York. If anyone at the Museum had anything to do with this, they could very easily have planted something of mine at the scene. I was the logical suspect anyway."

"My God, you don't think anyone at the Metropolitan is mixed up in this!"

"Who knows?"

"But they couldn't be. Anyway, the police *didn't* find anything of yours at Gould's apartment."

"How do you know they didn't?"

"Well, did they?"

"I don't know. I don't think so." Chandler got up from his chair, walked over to the porch railing, and stared out into the woods that began several hundred feet from the house.

"Do you mind if I ask you something, Alan?" Murray said.

"Go ahead, ask."

"Just what did happen between you and Gould before you left the Met?"

"What happened? We had an argument, that's what happened. I told him he hadn't any more right to be chairman of a department at a major museum than I have to be the King of Spain, if you want the general drift."

"That was a little narrow of you, Alan," Murray observed timidly.

"Narrow! Christ, the man was a complete nincompoop! He didn't know the first thing about design or composition or texture or anything. All he knew was psychology and a smattering of sociology—and a very sugary brand of those. He shouldn't have gone into art criticism, he should have been a goddamn social worker."

"Then why do you think you didn't get the job over Gould?"

"Oh, I don't know . . . he'd been there longer, I suppose."

"Is that the real reason?"

From his position at the railing, Chandler inspected Murray's face. "I wish I knew. You see, I have these stupid suspicions."

"What stupid suspicions?"

"Well, don't ask me why, but I have the feeling someone was trying to get me into a fight with Gould. The Director had read my work and he liked it. He liked it very much. He was always after me to send in articles to the journals. Then the curator resigned, Urqhart his name was. Nobody was very upset about that because the department had been too large anyway. They planned on not hiring any new people, just intended to appoint one of the present members as chairman. I honestly thought I might get the job. I know I was young and I'd only been there a year, but I thought that wouldn't matter. But when I saw the Director he acted completely differently from before. Not at all friendly or anything. He didn't even make any attempt to apologize or tell me how much the Museum valued my services. Nothing like, 'Stick around—the next vacancy that comes up, you'll get it,' nothing."

"Maybe you were the one with bad breath, not Gould," Murray suggested.

"Maybe," Chandler said absently. His eyes came to life again. "Anyway, someone, I have the feeling, turned the Director against me. Maybe it was Gould, and he just wanted the chairmanship very badly, but maybe"—he trained his eyes on Murray—"it was somebody who wanted the world to know that Gould and I weren't on the best of terms."

"Is that why you think someone at the Museum is involved in this? You think someone was trying to give you a motive for killing Gould?"

"I think it's possible. Oh, I admit it's pretty farfetched, but it's possible."

Murray was silent again. Then he said, "But you don't think the police found anything of yours in Gould's apartment. If a person wanted to frame you, it seems they would have been a little more obvious about it, especially since there was all that stuff of yours down in Emerson's office."

"Maybe whoever it was didn't know about that. Maybe they thought if they left something from that box in Gould's apartment it would be a little *too* obvious."

"Well," Murray said, "I'm beginning to understand your reasons for coming up here, at least. But I still think you should go to the police."

"With the world's prize motive for killing Gould?"

"But you don't have the world's prize motive. You didn't hate the man. You just disagreed with him intellectually."

"Exactly, but I'd like to see you explain that to a policeman. No, definitely not."

"Then what are you going to do?"

"Stay here until something happens."

"And lose your job at the Museum of Fine Arts?" Murray asked with concern.

"I'll tell them I've caught pneumonia. Let's talk about something else." Chandler was still looking out into the woods behind the house.

"What would you like to talk about?"

"Tell me what you think of everyone at the Met," Chandler said, turning around and trying to force his features into position for a smile.

Murray gave his impressions of the members of the department of European paintings, voicing scorn for Thalia Reynolds, awe for Elizabeth Mayer, amusement with Ferris, and lack of understanding of Emerson.

When he'd finished Chandler said, "Oh, by the way, what do you think of Sandy Janis? Nice, huh?"

Roger frowned. "I guess she's a sweet kid," he said lightly.

"Faint praise indeed," Chandler said. "Anything on between you two?"

"I've only been there a week and a half."

"Shouldn't take longer than that. For you." He grinned meaningfully.

Murray shrugged. "She's just a sweet kid."

"Okay."

"Listen, Alan," Murray said, becoming serious, "I have a feeling about Gould's murder."

"I'll listen."

"Well, did you hear about the robbery of Fischer's auction gallery?"

"I read something about it in the papers—I think it was in the same issue as the story of Gould's murder."

"That could be. I guess they didn't get it up here till the

next day. That robbery took place the same night Gould must have been killed. Either that or he was killed the morning after. I don't think they know exactly when it happened."

"And your theory is, the two incidents are connected."

"They must be."

"And this all has something to do with the Cézanne the Museum just bought from Fischer's too, I'll bet," Chandler said.

"As a matter of fact—"

"You're dreaming, Rodge. Probably one of Gould's old girl friends—and he must have had scads; he was quite good looking, you know, for a man of his age—one of them probably came back and shot him."

"I don't believe it," Murray said flatly. "And what's more I'm going to look into the matter of this robbery. Personally," he added, his eyes brightening. "You know, I was at Fischer's for the auction of the Cézanne—I guess I forgot to mention it—and a very interesting thing happened to me that evening."

"They auctioned off your trousers by mistake."

"Listen! for Christ's sake. I met the janitor of the place, and it turns out he found this pawn ticket on the floor the morning after the robbery. Now what I think is, it just might belong to the people who broke in during the night. Anyway, the janitor gave me the ticket and I'm going to follow it up."

"Do what you like," Chandler said, "but if you ask me I'd say you were wasting your time. The ticket probably belonged to one of the people who was visiting the gallery the day before."

"How many people do you know who frequent expensive auction galleries who also pawn things in pawnshops?"

"I suppose you might have a point there. It won't do any harm anyway."

"Harm? Look, Alan, at the moment you're suspect number one for the murder of Oscar Gould. If I can find out anything you might have reason to be very thankful."

"Maybe so," Chandler said resignedly. Then he snapped his fingers, waking himself out of a depression. "Say, have you eaten anything since you left New York?" he asked. "My God, you must be starved."

"I could use a sandwich maybe," Roger said.

"Sandwich, nothing. Follow me: you're about to sample some of the finest cooking in the White Mountains—and that's quite a sweeping statement, believe it or not."

They had a very large lunch, the high point of which was the clam chowder Aunt Mel had made the night before. Reheated, it was still a masterpiece. After lunch they went sightseeing, taking in all the typical tourist spots: the Old Man of the Mountains, the Presidential Range, and the Flume. Murray had missed these attractions on his last trip, and Chandler, being almost a native, had never seen them at all. At least he'd never taken the time to examine them closely.

Dinner surpassed lunch in both size and quality, and the two went to bed early. At ten-thirty the next morning Murray started up the engine of his Tempest, pulled out of the gravel parking lot, and headed back for New York.

SIX

THE WEDNESDAY AFTER MURRAY'S RETURN from New Hampshire started off as though it was going to be a normal day at the Met. The Cézanne had arrived on Monday, and on that day things had been in an uproar. Everyone wanted to get a look at the new picture. The registrar's storeroom, where all new acquisitions start out and remain until they've been catalogued and stamped with a number (the number is actually painted on to an inconspicuous corner of the piece), was the center of the confusion. Its large double doors had hardly a moment's rest the entire day. Even in corners of the Museum as remote as the department of Islamic art the Cézanne was the chief topic of conversation. Emerson went about his business that day with his face frozen into a look of venomous indignation; when anyone mentioned the Cézanne to him he stared past the speaker as if nothing had been said. He was like a middle-aged man forced to attend a teen-age party.

But on Tuesday everyone quieted down somewhat, and by Wednesday everything seemed to be back to normal.

Thalia Reynolds, the first one in the European paintings department after Murray and the secretaries, started in by complaining about her special-delivery package. "You're absolutely sure, now," she said, taking in both secretaries and Roger in her glance, "that none of you has gotten anything by mistake. It's a small square thing, probably."

All assured her they'd seen nothing like that around the office.

"Well, let me know if you see it," she said. "It's very important." She waved a finger at them and was gone.

Next came Emerson and Mrs. Mayer. "Honestly, George," she was saying, "I'm almost convinced you're right and Stanley Ferris is wrong. We don't need all those policemen in the lobby. We want to let people *see* the picture, don't we? And how can they if a big fat policeman is blocking their paths?"

"Just what I've been saying," Emerson said, shaking out his umbrella—it was doing something like sleeting outside—and struggling to get his rubbers off. "I'd like to have the picture just go on exhibit like any other picture, say opposite the big Monet in Gallery 38."

"That might be nice," Mrs. Mayer agreed. "I think I'll speak to Stanley Ferris about it myself. Is he here yet?"

"Miss Janis," Emerson said, between hops on his right foot —his left rubber was waging a terrific battle to stay on—"has Mr. Ferris been in this morning yet?"

"I don't think so. I haven't seen him," she said without looking up from her typewriter.

Emerson straightened up and said with exasperation, "Miss Janis."

"Yes?"

"Couldn't we manage a little more decorum?" He was staring at a spot near the base of her desk. Looking over there, Murray noticed one bare foot sticking out from behind the desk.

"My shoes are on the radiator," she said, pointing. "I stepped in a puddle." She looked at him helplessly.

"With both feet?" Emerson asked. There were two shoes on the radiator.

"Well, you wouldn't want me to walk around in one shoe, would you?"

"God forbid." Emerson sighed.

It had all the earmarks of a typical day. Then the phone rang.

Sandy picked it up and said, "European paintings." Then she said, "Yes, hold the wire a minute, would you?" She covered the mouthpiece. "Mr. Emerson, it's for you. It's Mount Sinai Hospital."

"Good God," Emerson said under his breath, "what kind of mess has Marge gotten herself into this time?" Marge was Emerson's wife who went around the country charging long-distance phone calls to her husband's private number. "I'll take it in my office, Miss Janis. Murray, could you, um, continue talking to Miss Janis for a few minutes?"

Emerson walked into his office and shut the door. Sandy pushed several buttons on the telephone console, and the faint sound of plastic on plastic was the last one to be heard in the reception room for several seconds. All eyes were on the door to Emerson's office.

Silence.

Then there was a muffled explosion from behind the door: "He's *what*!" More silence. Then: "Well, for the love of God, what happened?" A little later: "Well, could I speak to him?" in a more restrained voice. After that Emerson's words were unintelligible beyond the door.

Two minutes later he reemerged. Murray's, Sandy's, and Doris's eyes followed the smallest movements of his face, on which was a faraway, confused look. After some moments the curator swallowed and said, "Now don't anyone get excited. It's not as bad as it sounds."

All three started. "What's not as bad as it sounds?" Murray said with alarm, speaking for the group.

"Mr. Ferris has had an accident."

"What kind of accident?"

"Well," Emerson said slowly, "he's been shot . . ."

"Shot!" and "My God!" and "Oh no!" were heard from Murray, Sandy, and Doris respectively.

"Now wait a minute, wait a minute," Emerson said, pressing his palms against an imaginary wall in front of him, "he's not dead. In fact, they tell me he's not in any immediate danger. He's in a room in Mount Sinai—that's who that was. He should be out in a few days."

"What *happened*!" Sandy said. "How did it happen!"

"I didn't get all the details." Emerson rubbed a hand over his forehead. "Someone shot him this morning in his building."

"In his building!"

"Something about, he was coming out of his apartment and someone fired at him from behind. Hit him in the shoulder. That's all I got." He rubbed his forehead again, then switched over to rubbing the back of his neck. "Listen, Murray, I think you better get over there. Just so we can get the firsthand story, and avoid a lot of . . . rumors running around here," he said abstractedly.

"I'll get over there right away," Murray said.

"No, no, can't do that. Visiting hours don't start till two. Let's just . . . all try to collect ourselves for a few hours." And, shaking his head, he retired to his office once more.

As soon as the door was closed everyone started talking at once. "Who do you think . . ." "Why him?" "Why would anyone want to shoot Mr. Ferris?" "How could—"

"How in the world do you expect me to accomplish anything with a racket like this going on out here?" Thalia Reynolds was back. "What's all this chatter about, anyway?" She was standing in the archway to the vestibule that led to the other offices of the department, hands on hips.

"Mr. Ferris has been shot," Murray said timidly.

"Shot? Oh my God. *Oh* my God. First Oscar and now Stanley." She covered her eyes with her right hand.

"He's not . . . dead," Murray said.

"Not dead. Well, thank heavens for that, at least." She opened her mouth very wide and took a deep breath. "But, good grief, *why*? Are we the Mafia or something? Is this some sort of conspiracy?" Her eyelids ascended to an even higher level. "They might be after *all* of us! Anyone might be next! We need police protection. Someone call the police!" She swiveled her head from side to side and up and down. "I'm not feeling very well," she announced. "I think I'll just go inside and take something." And she, too, was gone.

It was near lunch time that Elizabeth Mayer heard about it. She first expressed sorrow, then sympathy for Mrs. Ferris, then she said to Murray, "I suppose you think the same person who killed Mr. Gould also shot Stanley Ferris."

Murray looked at her. Under the circumstances this seemed a strange thing to say. He said, "I hadn't really thought about it, but now that you mention it, it does appear as though it might have been the same man, yes."

"I feel that way myself. I'm not a detective, but look at the similarities: both shot in their own apartment buildings, both curators here. It doesn't take a genius to see it. But why do you think this person picked on those two?"

"Hmm?"

"I said why do you think Mr. Gould and Mr. Ferris were singled out? They've had plenty of time to try and kill the rest of us? Why just those two?"

"I never thought about it," Murray said. "Miss Reynolds thinks they're *going* to kill the rest of us."

"It's interesting, though," she said. "Well, let me know how Stanley is doing when you get back from the hospital, will you."

Murray said he would, and left for lunch. After a corned-beef sandwich in a Madison Avenue delicatessen, he wandered the streets idly, peering into the windows of expensive antique stores and art galleries. There seemed little sense in reporting back at the Museum before heading for the hospital, and he managed to kill time in this way until quarter to two. Then he started walking up Fifth Avenue toward Mount Sinai.

Entering through a revolving door, he inquired at a reception desk about Mr. Ferris. The woman behind the desk, who was not wearing a white nurse's uniform, checked her register and said, "Yes, let's see. Ferris. Right. Guggenheim Pavilion. Ninth floor. Room 915. Elevator to your right."

An allergy to verbs, Murray decided, riding up in the large automatic elevator. It was an occupational disease of receptionists. The elevator stopped at the ninth floor, and Murray started down the corridor. The hallway reeked hospital. Orderlies pushing stainless steel caddies scurried back and forth, darting into rooms. Interns all in white and residents with only a white jacket over their civilian clothes passed through, each with the prongs of a stethoscope protruding from a pocket or with the instrument around his neck. Everything—gray and white walls, linoleum-tiled floors, even standing ashtrays—was immaculate.

Murray soon found 915. The door was closed, and he knocked. There was no response from inside, and, standing before the door, he understood why. The water was running in the bathroom of the suite, and at a terrific rate. He knocked again, but it was clearly futile. He opened the door. Inside there was a single bed—nothing but a private room for Mr. Ferris, of course—half of which, the half near the head, was cranked up at a forty-five-degree angle. The water in the bathroom was still running furiously, but the door connecting the two rooms was slightly ajar.

"Mr. Ferris," Murray said. "MR. FERRIS. IT'S ME, ROGER MURRAY."

There was a sort of gurgle from the bathroom, the product of a mouth trying to form words while engaged in another activity. There was also a swishing noise, indicating that perhaps the activity was the brushing of teeth.

"MR. FERRIS," Murray shouted, "I WAS TERRIBLY SORRY TO HEAR ABOUT—"

"Gnngh," from the bathroom.

"I SAID, I WAS SORRY TO HEAR—HOW ARE YOU FEELING?"

"WOMMINNIT."

The water stopped running abruptly, and faint metallic noises could be heard from the bathroom. Murray felt a great sense of relief at the relative silence. In another few seconds

83

the bathroom door opened and a figure in a plaid cotton dressing gown came out. Over one arm was a towel.

"Mr. Ferris, I—" Murray focused his eyes on the figure. "You're not Mr. Ferris."

"And you're not my nephew Arthur Silverman from Cambridge, either. I don't know what this hospital's coming to. Can't a man have a little privacy while he's putting in his dentures?" said the figure, a thin, long-legged man with sunken cheeks, and he padded over to the bed and got into it without looking up at Murray again.

"I'm terribly sorry," Murray said. "This is the number they gave me downstairs. I'm terribly sorry," he repeated, and backed out of the room mumbling further apologies.

"A man can't have a moment's peace anymore," were the last words he heard from the man in the bed before he shut the door.

"Oh," said the girl at the reception desk when he confronted her again, "very sorry. That's *Feldman* in 915. Wrong number. Not Ferris at all. Let's see." She rechecked the register. "738A. That's Ferris. Silly mistake."

"738A—thank you," Murray said, in a tone devoid of gratitude, but the message was lost on the girl, who'd already gone back to the copy of *Cosmopolitan* magazine she had in her lap.

738A was a semiprivate room, one of whose two beds was indeed occupied by Mr. Ferris. In the other was a light-haired, middle-aged man, and by the side of his bed stood a boy of about ten with bright red hair and matching freckles. Mr. Ferris was sitting up in bed. He was wearing a pair of pale green hospital pajamas, several of whose buttons were unhooked, showing part of a large white bandage that encased his right shoulder. When Murray entered he was looking serenely through the window that ran the entire length of one wall of the room.

"Mr. Ferris," Murray said, with a mixture of alarm, surprise, and thanksgiving that he'd come to the right room.

"Hello there, Murray," Ferris said. "You really didn't have

to come all the way up here. It's not really serious, you know. What they call a flesh wound, I believe."

"Everybody's pretty worried about you," Murray said.

"Are you a cop?" the boy standing by the other bed asked in a matter-of-fact voice. He had turned to listen to the conversation. The man in the bed smiled helplessly.

Murray swung his head around. "No," he said.

"I'm just visiting my uncle," was the boy's reply to this.

"That's nice."

"'F you were a cop, you wouldn't *tell* me you were a cop, would you?"

"Probably not," Murray said.

"'S what I thought," the boy said with satisfaction.

Murray turned back to Mr. Ferris. "What happened to you? Mr. Emerson didn't quite get all the details."

"It's a long story," Ferris said. "Have a seat."

Murray sat down in an aluminum tube chair with vinyl cushions and rounded corners, and Ferris launched into his story. As he'd been leaving his apartment this morning he'd sensed a rush of air by his ear and a thump against the wall behind him, as though someone had hit it with a rubber-tipped mallet. He spun around but saw no one in back of him. There was another whizz and another thump, no loud explosions, and Ferris soon put two and two together and acknowledged that, strange as it seemed, someone was shooting at him with a gun equipped with a silencer. After the second shot there had been a slight ricochet sound, if without the singing tones common in Western movies, and the noise was what had convinced him finally.

He panicked.

There were two choices. He could try to reopen the door of his apartment, an alternative that would involve fishing his house key out of his key case, which in turn had to be fished out of his pocket, or he could make for the back stairway. He decided for the stairway. He started running toward it, and then a third hiss sounded. He felt a sharp sting in his right shoulder. The pain seemed to rush outward from that part of his body, as if traveling through his veins. He looked down at the shoulder of his suit jacket and noticed a red stain growing there. At this point he lost consciousness. "A case of vasovagal syncope," the doctor said later, not bothering to translate. The doctor also informed Ferris that the bullet had missed his collarbone by about half an inch, and, that being the case, he would probably be out in "a day or two."

"Did you find out who brought you to the hospital?" Murray asked.

"Man down the hall found me lying there, evidently, and called the police. He probably saved my life."

"I thought the wound wasn't that serious."

Ferris chuckled. "Wouldn't have died from *that* wound," he said. "But it certainly looks like this gunman was out to kill me, and if this man down the hall hadn't come along when he did—that was right after the shot that hit me was fired—well, the man with the pistol could have come over and finished me off. At least, that's the way the police see it."

"They've spoken to you already, the police."

"Soon as I regained consciousness, there they were."

"Did they tell you anything? Have they any clues?"

"They only opened their mouths to breathe, and they didn't even do very much of that. I did all the talking."

"Didn't they even tell you if they thought the same people who killed Mr. Gould are the ones who shot at you?"

"I didn't trouble to ask," Ferris said. "It seems plain as day they're the same ones."

"I know where their hideout is," sang the freckle-faced boy by the other bed.

Murray turned to him. "Whose hideout?"

"The crooks' hideout, the crooks that shot the other man." He pointed to Ferris. "They're right downstairs every night. Their hideout's in the room right underneath this one." He bounced up and down a couple of times in celebration of the fact.

"I'm afraid you're making a big mistake," Murray explained

to the boy patiently. "The man in the bed here isn't shot. He's in the hospital for an appendectomy."

"An appen-what?" said the boy, but his fire had fizzled, and he clearly didn't expect an answer.

Murray pulled his chair a little closer to Ferris's bed, lowered his voice, and said, "You see, the reason I asked, everyone at the Museum is kind of worried that somebody may be trying to kill off the entire European paintings staff."

"I doubt it. They've had plenty of time to try for the others, but they haven't. What I can't understand is why they should have tried to kill only me and Gould."

"Mrs. Mayer said the same thing," Murray remarked. "I can't see any reason. Do you suppose it might have something to do with the Cézanne?"

"I don't see how it could. About the only thing Gould and I had in common with respect to the picture is that we both *saw* it. What difference could that make?"

Murray shook his head. "I don't see how it could make any." He looked at his watch. "I suppose I ought to be on my way. Mr. Emerson's going to be wondering what happened to me."

"Tell everyone I'm fine and not to worry. Should be back in a couple of days at the most."

"I will."

"Say," the boy by the other bed piped up as Murray was opening the door to leave, "dja ever think maybe this picture you're talking about might have microfilm hidden in it? Could be there's Russian spies trying to get it to their agents in this country."

Murray looked deliberately over his shoulder and glowered at the boy. Then his face relaxed. "Oh, that," he said. "We've already found the microfilm. Must be something else."

"You *found* the microfilm?" The boy's eyes were huge. "What did you do with it?"

"What does one always do with microfilm?" Murray said with elaborate disinterest. "Swallowed it, of course."

And he closed the door behind him.

The following morning, which was a Thursday, Murray decided to wear his good suit to work. A long train of thought had preceded this decision. On his way home from work the afternoon before, he'd talked to another girl on the street. She wasn't any better than the one he'd spoken to in Central Park, but she had nevertheless given him hope that this method of meeting people might eventually produce results. She was about a Three and a Half. Soon after he'd first started talking to strange girls in public places, he'd settled on a system of classification. A One was a girl who prompted a single careful inspection. A Two he might examine a second time. A Three was someone he might make an attempt to speak to—if conditions were auspicious. There was a chance he would call up a Four and ask her out for a drink. (He'd encountered only two of these so far, and he hadn't called them.) A Five was someone he could have a serious relationship with—at least temporarily. (All the Fives he'd ever met had been introduced to him by friends, and he was beginning to wonder if such girls ever went out on the street or into supermarkets.) And a Six—well, he had yet to meet a Six. But on this particular morning, having been encouraged by the Three and a Half of the previous afternoon, he had the feeling this might be the day. So he put on his good suit.

It was the suit he'd worn to the auction a week ago, and as he was depositing his keys, change, and wallet in the pants pockets he came upon something in the front, right-hand pocket. It was the pawn ticket stub the cleaning man at Fischer's had entrusted to him that night, on the promise he would redeem it. With the confusion owing to the Cézanne's arrival at the Museum and Ferris's accident he'd forgotten about it. He looked at the front of the ticket. Underneath the words *Universal Security Loan Co.* was an address on Second Avenue. With a determined nod he resolved to investigate the place during his lunch hour. For one thing, he was dying to know if the ticket had any connection with the robbery—or with any of these murders and attempted murders—and for another, he thought this might just possibly be destiny's way of making contact with him.

88

You never knew when the owner of a pawnshop was going to turn out to be a Six.

It was twelve-fifteen when Emerson dismissed him, and without eating anything first Murray walked to the Seventy-seventh Street station of the Lexington Avenue IRT subway. He boarded a downtown train and was soon heading across Union Square toward Second Avenue. Murray had some familiarity with the area, having accompanied his brother on used-book-buying jaunts on several occasions—the used-book district of New York is just south of Union Square—and, according to his calculations, the pawnshop was somewhere between Eighth and Fourteenth streets. He found it on the block between Ninth and Tenth.

The Universal Security Loan Co. was a small, sleazy, ancient place. Heavy-gauge grating protected its windows at all times and its door at night from the inevitable vandals. Above the door was the traditional pawnshop insignia—three gold balls. Sometimes, Murray felt, it was a genuine source of comfort to come across something in real life that so conformed to its stereotype. The inside was dimly lit, perhaps with a good deal of foresight on the part of the owner. This way, a customer had to depend on his nose to sense the general air of dilapidation. Glass cases lined up on either side of the store were filled with objects whose most striking feature was their second-handness—tarnished saxophones, dusty press cameras, plating-eroded jewelry, rusty hunting rifles. Altogether, a very depressing place.

The owner, Murray was quick to recognize, was no Six—not even a Three. He was a solidly built man of about sixty, nearly bald on top but in need of a shave below, and he wore a complicated set of eyeglasses, which looked like two or three pairs hinged together. As Murray entered he was seated at a workbench behind one of the counters. Without rising, he flipped up one pair of the hinged glasses and said, "Now wait a minute, wait a minute, don't tell me. You're looking for something nice in a violin." He smiled expectantly, showing very poor teeth.

89

"No. Actually," Murray said, delving into his pocket, "I've got a ticket here."

"You're kidding me," said the proprietor. "You want to redeem?"

"Yes."

"That's funny. I distinctly see you as a violinist. But . . ." He shrugged. "You want to redeem, you want to redeem. Let me see what you've got there."

Murray handed over the ticket. The owner examined it, looked at the reverse side (which was blank), bobbed his head in a kind of figure eight, and walked off to the rear of the store. Thirty seconds later he was back lugging a large wooden contraption with both arms. At first it seemed to be nothing more than a bunch of paint-stained laths joined together haphazardly. Then the owner set it down and Murray saw what it was—an easel, a painter's easel. Well, that looked like something.

"There y'are, Jack," said the owner. "For ten bucks she's all yours."

Murray pulled out his wallet and was about to extract a ten-dollar bill when a thought occurred to him. If he merely paid for the thing he'd have one mangy-looking easel on his hands and he'd be not a step closer to the solutions of any of the problems that were worrying him. Somehow he had to elicit information about the man who had pawned the easel. This man, he was sure, was in some way tied in with the robbery at Fischer's, at the very least, if not with the two shootings.

With his hand on the bill Murray paused and looked up at the pawnshop owner. "Uh, there's a slight problem here," he said.

The owner nodded vigorously. "Ah, I get it, I get it. You don't really want the easel, is that it? You're really looking for something else."

"No, no," Murray said, "I'd like the easel. The problem is, it's not really *my* easel, you see. It belongs to a friend. A . . . friend of a friend, really. And he asked me to pick it up for his friend, that is, my friend asked me—"

"Hold on a minute, hold on. I'm not so good at higher mathematics. Just what is it you want from me?"

"Well, all I need is the address of the person who pawned the easel to begin with. You see, my friend lost the address—"

"Wait, wait, let's not start with the friend business again. Look, you want the address, I got it, you can have it. For ten dollars you get the easel *and* the address. How's that?"

Murray smiled and gave the man his money.

The proprietor left the easel with Murray and crossed over to the other side of the store to check his files. Humming tunelessly, he flipped through one drawer of a small metal file cabinet, pushing the cards back and forth with nimble fingers. After a minute or two he pulled one of the cards out and came back over to Murray. "Got it right here," he said. "Can't quite make out the first name, though. Hamilton, I think, or Harrison—I think it's Harrison. Last name—Smith. You got a pencil? You'll have to copy it; I can't let you have the card."

Murray found a ball-point pen in his shirt pocket and copied the information:

Harrison Smith
17 Morton Street

"You all set now?" the owner asked when he'd finished writing. "Don't forget the easel."

Murray didn't forget it. All the way back uptown on the IRT he was unintentionally jabbing standees on the toes with it. But the trip hadn't been a total loss. He had something—something that was probably insignificant, it was true—but at least something. And, he thought, smiling up at the ceiling of the subway car, it was a piece of information the police very likely didn't know about.

SEVEN

"I HOPE YOU DON'T THINK you're going to keep that thing around here," Ira said as Murray entered the apartment carrying the easel. "I run a very tight house."

"*You* run?" said Martha from the kitchen where she was setting the table for dinner. "Listen to him." She came into the living room. "Personally, I think it's a fine idea for you to take up painting, Roger," she said when she saw the easel.

Roger regarded her curiously. "Who said anything about—"

"Painting!" Ira exclaimed. "Oh no, o-o-oh no. Now listen to me, Rodge. You're a critic, you understand that? Your job is to write, to analyze, to interpret. Why, without people like you—"

"Wait a second," Roger said. "Hold on a second, you two. I'm not taking up painting."

"Then what in the world are you doing with that thing?" Ira asked. "What's it doing here?" He inspected the easel while Roger was setting it against a wall. "You know, actually, Rodge," he said thoughtfully, "if you don't want it, I think I could make some nice bookshelves out of it. For right over

. . . there, I think." He gazed speculatively at some blank wall space to Roger's right.

Murray tilted his head and hunched his shoulders in parodied magnanimity. "Be my guest, Ira baby," he said, extending his arms. "Grind it up and make toilet paper if you like. I won't stop you."

"Never mind." Ira tramped over to the couch and picked up the day's copy of the *Wall Street Journal.*

"Where *did* you get it, Roger?" Martha asked, after a reproving look at her husband.

"Well, you remember the night I went to that auction? When the Museum bought the Cézanne? Well, I met the janitor of the auction gallery that night, and he gave me this pawn ticket. You see, he found it the morning after the robbery they had there. So I went down—"

Ira's head sprang up. "Don't tell me you're doing some more detective work, Rodge."

"Well, it might be important."

Ira clicked his tongue. "You know, I don't know what I'm going to do about you. I remember—do you remember this, Rodge?—I remember, when you were little you had this *thing.* You know, Martha, how most boys want to be policemen or firemen—or rock-and-roll singers—when they grow up? Not Roger. He wanted to be an ambassador. You remember that, Rodge?"

"Vaguely."

"I have to tell Martha. Listen to this, Martha. You see, Roger was just a little kid, maybe eight or nine, at the time. And he was standing around one day when somebody—I think it was Uncle Herman—was saying to somebody else, 'Well, if you don't like it in this country, why don't you move to Brooklyn?' So Roger said right away, 'Can I go too?' And Uncle Herman—if it was Uncle Herman—said, 'Go? Kid, you can be the ambassador.' And after that, you went around everywhere saying you were going to be an ambassador, and when someone asked, 'The ambassador to where?' you said, 'Brooklyn.' "

"What is this little parable intended to prove?" Roger asked dryly.

"That you're always flying off on tangents," Ira replied. "That you have to be a little more rational in your behavior, a little more realistic about life."

"Sometimes the confidence a man has in his kid brother is truly heartwarming."

"Oh, you know what I mean, Rodge," Ira said. "You have to just buckle down."

"Well, I disagree," Martha said. "I think Roger should do what he likes. Why shouldn't he—"

"*Uh,*" Ira interrupted, laboriously consulting his watch, "isn't it almost time for dinner, sweetiepie?"

Martha shot Ira a glare filled with the fury that hell hath none like, clamped her lips together, wheeled, and strode into the kitchen.

"Ira, Ira, Ira," Murray said when she'd gone. "My own brother Ira."

On Friday, Roger said nothing to anyone about the easel. By five o'clock he was ready to burst with the news. He and Sandy were the last two left in the office. As he walked past her desk on his way out he said, "Well, have a good weekend," and realized he was going to have to keep bottled up for the next two days.

"If you could just wait one second," she said as he was heading for the door, "I'll walk out with you. I just have to type this one thing and I'll be done." She added, "And I'm a little afraid to go out of here alone right now with all these . . ."

"I'll wait," Roger said, grinning over at the top of her head.

On the way out he told her about his discovery of the pawn ticket and the redemption of it. She expressed great interest, and when he mentioned the easel her mind began to work at full steam. "Maybe the thief was a budding young artist, and he had to sell his supplies to buy burglarizing equipment. He probably has this *huge* family to support." She smoothed down an imaginary page in the air. "I see about twelve kids."

"Yes, well, I guess it's possible."

They had reached the corner of Seventy-ninth and Fifth. Sandy came to a stop and said, "Well, I'd love to continue this conversation, but I'm afraid this is where I get off. I catch the Seventy-ninth Street Crosstown bus."

Roger looked into her face for a second or two, realized he was staring, and pretended to make a quick survey of the rush-hour traffic. "If you're really interested we could have dinner together," he said. "I mean . . ."

"Is that supposed to be an invitation, Mr. Murray? I must say it's a little hard to tell from the tone of your voice alone."

"Oh, I know it's Friday night. You probably have all sorts of commitments and things."

"Well, it so happens I do have one. To my roommate. I could always call her, of course. She's very understanding about these things. But if you're going to make it sound like a few hours on the rack . . ."

"No, no, I really do want to take you out for dinner. The only thing is, well, I'm a little short of funds at the moment . . ."

She smiled and light came to her eyes. "Well, if that's really all it is I know a nice little place. Come on," she said. "I can even pay if you want."

Murray stood there for a minute looking puzzled. Then he said, "Oh, you don't have to pay. As long as it's not one of these terrifically overpriced places."

"Everything in New York's overpriced, but this one's less overpriced than most. Come on."

The restaurant she had in mind was the London Pub on Madison Avenue between Seventy-seventh and Seventy-eighth. It was a very small combination bar and short-order dining room. You went down three very old oak steps and found yourself in almost complete darkness. A dim red glow came from the bar, but in the dining area there were only the jar candles on the tables for illumination. When Murray's eyes became accustomed to the dark he was barely able to distinguish that the style of the place was Old English.

Waiters paraded around in red coats, and everything was stone fireplaces and beamed ceilings.

Roger and Sandy took seats opposite one another in a booth, and very shortly a waiter was thrusting menus in front of them and saying, "Here y' are, guv."

"How do they expect us to read these?" Murray asked.

"I'll read it to you," Sandy said. "It says, 'Roaft lamb with mint dreffing, Falifbury fteak . . .'"

"I get the picture. What would you like?"

"I think I'll have the fteak."

As if he'd been eavesdropping (as if?), the red-coated waiter appeared almost at once. "Ready to order, guv?" he asked. "What'll it be?"

"I don't suppose you have anything like firefly stew," Murray said, but when he noticed that the waiter's expression hadn't changed he became sedate, gave Sandy's order, and after a moment of indecision said, "Better make that two." Sandy was giggling quietly.

The waiter disappeared into the blackness. When he was out of range Sandy said, "You know, I feel badly about this. Sort of like I forced you to take me out for dinner."

"Bad," Roger corrected. "You feel *bad*, and forget about the dinner."

"There you go again correcting people. I've noticed you do that quite a lot. You seem to be very outgoing, but actually I have the feeling that, deep down, you're a very shy person. You compensate for it by making clever remarks and correcting people."

"Listen, I don't mind taking you out for dinner—I've said that—but if I'm going to be psychoanalyzed into the bargain I might begin to mind."

"I'm only trying to help you understand yourself. I feel it's more or less impossible to function as a person until you really know yourself."

Murray couldn't prevent himself from smiling. "Oh, you do, do you?"

"I think so, yes. But, look, if it's going to make you uncomfortable to discuss these things frankly and openly, let's talk about something else." Without waiting for him to respond she said, "What do you think about these murders?"

"There's only been one murder," he reminded her. "And that was somebody I haven't even met."

"You should have, he was quite something—very handsome. In a way," she added as an afterthought. "Do you think anyone at the Museum is mixed up in all this?"

That was the second time he'd been asked that. He looked straight at her and said, "Why? Do you think so?"

"I don't know," she replied. "But there sure have been some strange things going on over there."

"What kind of strange things?"

She ran her finger around the rim of the water glass on the table in front of her. "Well, for one thing, there's this package Miss Reynolds keeps talking about. She's very anxious about it. Wants to make sure no one else gets their hands on it before she does."

"What do you think it is?"

"I don't know, but I think it has something to do with all this business. She knows Mrs. Aldeburg, the widow of the former owner of the Cézanne, you know."

"That doesn't sound very incriminating. What do you think's in the package?"

"I haven't the vaguest idea," Sandy said. "It hasn't come yet. From the way she describes it, it sounds like it's a small square box, maybe flat. What do you think that could mean?"

"Almost anything. What other strange things have you noticed?"

Sandy lined up her place mat, which had gone slightly askew, with the edge of the table. "Well, this happened a couple of months ago, but I thought it was very strange. Mr. Emerson started getting these phone calls."

"Phone calls?"

"Yes. The strange thing is that they were all long distance, usually from someplace in Connecticut. That's the funny part: they came from all different places."

"Who were they from?" Murray asked.

"I don't know. You see, I took the calls in the office, and

I only spoke to the long-distance operator. They were all person-to-person. Whoever it was who was calling didn't say a word until Mr. Emerson came on the line."

"Is he still getting these calls?"

"No. I think they stopped just before Mr. Gould became chairman and Alan Chandler lost his job. I've heard rumors you're a friend of his, by the way."

"I am, sort of." Murray considered for a time. "What makes you think there's anything suspicious in all this?"

"Just a feeling I have. Whenever Emerson came on the line, he spoke very low. But occasionally he became very excited and said things like 'Goddamnit, stop this,' or 'I can't take this anymore.'"

"And he got these calls at the *office*?" Murray asked.

"That's right."

The waiter, bearing several plates on a tray, was heading back in their direction. He transferred the plates to the table, said mechanically, "Hope you enjoy the food, guv," and was off again to his other customers.

Murray stared down at the plate before him. The Salisbury steak, outweighed by runny mashed potatoes and watery peas, looked as though it was not among friends on the dish, but he decided to say nothing about it to Sandy. "Well, it looks very . . . interesting."

"The steaks have shrunk, I think, since the last time I was here," she said apologetically.

"They've been out there in the kitchen that long, huh?"

"You're being nasty again."

They ate in silence until Murray couldn't stand the noise of silverware on porcelain any longer. "So what do you think I should do about this pawn ticket?" he asked, after swallowing a hunk of what the restaurant called steak.

"You've got the address," she answered. "Why don't you go down there and see who lives at the place?"

"I suppose I could do that." His face suddenly brightened. "Say, are you doing anything this evening?" he asked.

"I'd love to," she said.

Seventeen Morton Street was one of those old buildings

that have, once upon a time, been town houses but have since been cut up into small apartments. Owing to the nature of their creation, these units frequently have such barbarities as windowless (and nearly doorless) kitchens and bathrooms that open off living rooms. While their outsides, occasionally ivy-covered, have remained pretty much intact over the years their insides have deteriorated to a hair-raising condition; possibly because the occupants, mostly students, have no interest in maintaining them. Normally, they contain little or no furniture.

This particular building was one of the smaller such, three stories high with one tenant on each floor. In any event there was room for one; two of the mailboxes lacked nameplates. The third had the name *J. D. Wollman* emblazoned on it in a homemade but professional-looking calligraphy. Underneath the name was the additional information "Apt. 1."

There was no outer door, and Roger and Sandy quickly found a door in the small first-floor hallway with a large nueral "1" painted on it. (Down along the same wall was another door with the legend *Back Door* in the same florid script that appeared on the mailbox.) Murray knocked. A girl's voice came through the door: "Who is it?"

Murray spoke. "We're looking for a man named Harrison Smith. Does he live in the building, do you know?"

"Not in this apartment. Didn't you read the sign on the mailbox?"

"We thought you might be able to tell us which apartment's his. He doesn't have his name out there."

Sounds of locks being unlocked. In a few seconds a girl waring faded blue jeans and a man's Oxford shirt, tails out, opened the door. She had long, flowing dark hair that completely obscured one eye. The girl's face went through a variety of expressions: bewilderment, curiosity, amusement. "Hey, wow," she said, "you're not from the Internal Revenue Service, are you?"

"Not really, no . . ." Murray mumbled.

"*What?*" said the girl. It was like a gunshot. Perhaps she was slightly hard of hearing.

"No," he said, louder, "we're not official at all."

"Oh." She was distinctly disappointed. "Hey, wow, I had a theory about Mr. Harry Smith. I figured the government must be after him for tax evasion."

"Why do you say that?" Murray asked.

"Because of the way he moved out of here. Sort of like, stole away in the middle of the night. One day he was here, the next day he was gone. Weird, you know."

"He's completely moved out then."

"Oh, yes."

"Did you know Mr. Smith very well?" Sandy asked.

"Not at all, practically. I'm not even sure which one was him. Hey, wow, I don't like to make you stand in the hall like this. Why don't you come in, sit down for a while. I was just taking a break from my 'Spirit of Peace Confronting Richard Nixon' anyway."

"Your what?" Murray said, following her inside. Sandy wound up the procession.

"'Spirit of Peace Confronting—'"

"That's what I thought you said. What is it?"

J. D. Wollman motioned their gaze over to a corner of the living room. The living room itself was a starkly decorated affair, but in this corner stood a large sheet-metal and wire conglomeration. It consisted of two main lumps: one a tangled mass of wire—coils and curlicues—the other a more orderly array of straight lines of wire stretched across sheet-metal lyre frames. The orderly array of wire was on the right; both components were set up on a wooden platform.

"I sculpt," she explained. "That's Nixon on the left, in case you were wondering."

"Interesting," Murray said.

"Do you do this for a living?" Sandy asked.

"It's the only work I do," she said evasively. "I haven't actually sold anything yet. But someday you ought to be hearing the name Judy Wollman."

Murray put on an inquisitive look and pointed at her.

"That's me," she said.

"I'm Roger Murray," Murray said. "This is Sandy Janis. We're from the Metropolitan."

"Museum?"

"That's the one."

"Hey, wow, I'm sure glad you people stopped by."

"Actually," Murray said, "we're not authorized to buy, this trip, you see. We're just looking."

"Anyway," Sandy remarked, "I can see your work's much too advanced for us. We're very stodgy."

Judy Wollman looked somewhat disappointed again, but she managed to say, "Are you interested in Harry Smith's stuff upstairs?"

"Is he an artist?" Murray asked eagerly.

"Like I told you, I don't even know which one he was. So many people used to come and go up there. I did see this broad-shouldered guy once. Gave me a dirty look as he was going up the stairs. That might have been Harry Smith, but if it was he sure didn't look like any artists I've ever known."

"What did he look like?"

"Kind of stupid face. Clumsy. But strong, you know. Say, why are you people so interested in Harry Smith? He done something wrong? I kind of suspected he was trafficking in stolen diamonds." She walked over to the metal sculpture and polished a facet of it with her fingertip.

"We're just . . . curious," said Sandy.

"*What?*" Judy Wollman blasted.

"We think," Murray said, "he's behind a plot to assassinate the Sanitation Commissioner."

"Hey, wow, that's great," she said listlessly, staring fixedly at her sculpture. "You know, I think another wire lengthwise on the right . . ."

"Which apartment did you say he used to live in?" Murray asked in a stentorian voice.

"What? Oh. Both of them," she said.

"Both?"

"Yeah, he had the two top floors all to himself."

"Was it a business or something?"

"I really couldn't say."

"When did he move out?"

"Week or two ago. I don't remember exactly." She was still concentrating on the sculpture. She pulled herself around abruptly and faced Roger and Sandy. "Hey, wow, I just had an inspiration. I'll have to get back to work now. You people are welcome to stay and watch if you like."

"Thanks, but"—Murray fumbled at his left sleeve—"it's getting late, and we have to be going." His eyes pointed the way to the door to Sandy.

"Yes, we do," she said.

"Hey, wow," said Judy Wollman, "I hope you find Harry Smith." She wasn't bothering to see them out. Instead she gradually crept over toward the metal sculpture while they sidled in the other direction to the door. In Murray's last vision of her through the doorframe she was about to pounce.

Out in the hall he said to Sandy, "A very interesting girl."

"Hey, wow, you're right," she said.

"Now *you're* being nasty."

Sandy let out a lungful of air and said, "Well, I guess it's back home."

"Back home, hell, we're going to see what the upstairs looks like." Almost automatically he took her hand. Several seconds later he became aware he was holding it, and without looking back at her face, he dropped it. "Come on," he said with unexpected force, and started up the drooping wooden stairs to the second floor.

On the landing there were two more doors, placed in the same relative positions as those to Judy Wollman's apartment below. But here they were painted a bright yellow instead of the orange-pink of the ones on the first floor. Roger knocked on the one nearer the front of the building, but the attempt was clearly useless. There was no light showing through the crack above the threshold, and no sounds whatsoever from the other side of the door. He gave the handle several turns, but also to no avail.

"We could try the one upstairs," Sandy suggested.

But they had no more luck here than on the second floor. "Well, I guess it is back home," Murray said dejectedly.

Sandy's eyebrows slanted up, and a pained smile came to her lips. "Why don't we go back to my house for coffee?" she said. "Cheer you up."

"Won't your roommate be asleep?"

"God, let's hope so," Sandy said, with her happiest look of the evening.

The roommate turned out to be better than asleep: she was out. Sandy made instant coffee, and the two of them talked for an hour and a half—about nothing in particular: Chandler, Murray's college experiences, the people at the Museum, Sandy's assortment of ex-roommates and their idiosyncrasies—until Murray glanced at his watch and saw that it was suddenly twelve-thirty. With as much enthusiasm as he could muster, in his state of nearly total exhaustion, he thanked her, told her that he'd really had an enjoyable evening, and left.

The next day a surprising thing occurred, the surprising part occurring in his mind. He was walking down Madison Avenue on his way to nowhere when he noticed an astonishingly beautiful girl peering into the window of a swanky clothing store. She was clearly in no hurry to get to anywhere either, and the circumstances couldn't have been more favorable. But he stared at her long enough to allow her to lose interest in the window and move on without his having made the slightest attempt to talk to her. What was going on here? Didn't he *want* to talk to her?

And he remembered Judy Wollman from the night before. Not the type of girl he was likely to marry, perhaps, but why didn't he even consider calling her? Was he losing his nerve in his old age or what?

Interesting. Very interesting.

EIGHT

MONDAY MORNING Murray recalled the two facts Sandy had told him about over dinner on Friday, and he thought about the possibilities of investigating them further. There was probably no way in the world to ask Mr. Emerson directly about the mysterious phone calls, he conceded, but he thought he might be able to devise a way to inquire unobtrusively about Thalia Reynolds's package. He was saved the trouble of inventing a pretext to go and see her when Emerson sent him to her office a little before eleven.

When he entered she was sitting at her desk, her chin resting on her right hand and a sheaf of papers before her. She jumped a little as Murray opened the door—not having bothered to knock—and said, "Oh, it's you, Mr. Murray."

He apologized incoherently for breaking in. Then he said, "Mr. Emerson wanted to know if you had the final list for the Summer Loan Exhibit."

"I don't have it," she replied, somewhat taken aback, as though he'd made an accusation. "I think Elizabeth, uh, Mrs. Mayer's going over it right now."

"I'll ask her." He was in the process of turning around to leave when she spoke again.

"Tell her I'd like to take another look at it when she's finished, will you."

"I'll do that. By the way," he said cautiously, "Sandy Janis said you were expecting some sort of package in the mail."

Thalia Reynolds looked him up and down curiously and with a suggestion of distaste. "I was," she said meaningly.

"But you're not anymore."

"No." She let her glance fall to the papers on the desk, but after a short interval she raised her head again abruptly. "What has this to do with you, Mr. Murray?"

He waved his hands and tried to adopt an expression of Garden-of-Eden innocence. "Nothing," he said. "I was just wondering if it came, that's all. Thought I'd look out for it if you wanted me to."

"How kind, but it's already arrived."

"It has?" He was unable to stifle his eagerness.

"Yes. It was from Mrs. Aldeburg, in fact."

"The widow of the man who owned the Cézanne?" There was no point in trying to control himself. She was clearly going to tell him the entire story, and his only misgiving was with regard to why she had chosen to disclose the information to him.

"The same," she said majestically. "You see, several days after James Aldeburg died—this was before that chicken hawk Albert Fischer had purchased the picture—Mrs. Aldeburg thought someone broke into her house."

"Thought?"

"She wasn't sure because she only heard noises during the night, and when she checked over everything in the morning nothing was missing. Besides, they had a very extensive burglar alarm system that went off when someone stepped on the floor of the living room. They only turned it on at night, of course." She smiled dimly. "In any case it didn't go off during the night, but when Mrs. Aldeburg went down in the morning one of the windows in the living room was open. As

I say, there was nothing missing, so she didn't report it to the police."

"And this package?"

"Patience, Mr. Murray. A little later the next day one of the gardeners found a roll of film on the front lawn just below the living room window that was found open. There were also a lot of footprints around, and Mrs. Aldeburg thought that this roll of film might have been dropped by the person who had tried to break in. I spoke to her very shortly after all this, and I persuaded her to send me the film."

"Why didn't she take it to the police?"

"Mrs. Aldeburg, I'm afraid, doesn't like the police. Something I think she picked up from her late husband. She asked me if I would take care of the matter. Discreetly."

Murray scratched an area behind his left ear and then put both hands in his pockets hurriedly. "What was on the film?" he asked.

"Nothing."

"Nothing?"

"The film was unexposed." Thalia Reynolds sighed. "I don't suppose it's really very important, after all."

"Oh, I think it might be very important," Murray said fervently.

"There was one interesting thing," Thalia Reynolds said offhandedly.

"What was that?"

"It was color film. A very high grade of commercial color film."

At two o'clock that afternoon Murray was passing through the reception room when he heard Sandy say, "Roger, do you think you could give me a hand with this?" She was hunched over the long fluorescent lamp that stood on the left side of her desk.

"What?" he said, halting in the center of the room.

"Come over here, stupid, and I'll show you."

One of the fluorescent tubes of the lamp had burned out, she explained. The custodian had brought up a new tube but had merely left it sitting on her desk inside its box, and installation of the new tube was a project well beyond her manual capabilities. "I was lucky to get the box open," she said. "I'm about as mechanical as a chimpanzee."

"Chimpanzees are very mechanical," Roger pointed out. "Do you know that if you put a banana a few feet above a chimpanzee's reach and put two sticks in his cage—"

"You're doing it again," she said in a tired monotone.

"Sorry. Let me see the lamp."

While he was fooling around with the fixture, Sandy said, "You know, I think we ought to go back to that Morton Street place again. There might be a fire escape around the back of the building, and we might be able to get a look at the upstairs apartments through a window."

His head was curled around, so that he was looking underneath the metal shade at the socket. Without shifting position he said, "Are you suggesting we break in?"

"No. We could just look through the window."

"Suppose the shades are down."

"Then that's the way the cookie crumbles. But they might very well be up."

He uncurled his head and stared straight at her. "Empty apartments always have the shades down," he said flatly.

"God, I don't know how you're ever going to get through life with an attitude like that."

"I've made it"—he gave a slight grunt as he pushed the tube into place—"this far."

"You've been lucky."

"Could be. Anyway, it's all done." He indicated the lamp.

"You're a genius," she said, smiling warmly.

That evening Ira and Martha were both out. Ira was working late, and Martha was attending a class in Eastern religions she took at the New School. Murray made a TV dinner, helped himself to a tall brandy from Ira's reserves, and settled down on the couch to think. He'd thought for about fifteen minutes when he suddenly pulled himself to his feet and went to the closet to get his coat. In another twenty minutes, after a short bus ride, he was on the IND heading downtown.

Seventeen Morton Street looked very much the same as it had the night before except that tonight Judy Wollman's light was out, so that all the building's front windows were dark. Murray gazed despairingly at the front façade for a couple of seconds before starting down the narrow alley to the left of the apartment house. At the rear there was a small paved courtyard bounded by a high wooden fence, and beyond the fence was a similar courtyard for the building that faced onto the next street after Morton.

Murray reached into his pocket and pulled out the small flashlight he'd had the foresight to bring along. (It was the device by which Ira was able to read his philosophy books in bed while Martha was trying to fall asleep.) He shone the light on the rear façade of the building, and, lo and behold, there was a fire escape. But that wasn't especially surprising in view of the fire laws of the City of New York. He moved the dim spot the flashlight was producing down the length of the scaffolding. About ten feet above the ground the spot suddenly slid onto blank brick wall. He blinked and moved the light back up again, halting it when it first fell on metalwork again.

Moving the flashlight spot back and forth across the bottom of the scaffolding, he realized what the situation was. The structure had apparently been designed with just such visitors as Murray in mind. The fire escape had ladders connecting the balcony on each floor with the one on the floor below—except on the second floor. Here there was a retractable ladder that was kept horizontal, probably by some spring mechanism, until someone pushed it down from above.

He slapped his hands against his sides, shook his head, and began to turn around. But halfway through the turn he held up. Switching on the flashlight again, he ran the dim spot along the bottom edge of the rear wall. A diverse collection of odds and ends had accumulated here over the years—bedsprings, bicycle wheels, wood laths—and Murray thought there was a chance he might be able to find something among the rubble with which to pull down the last stage of the fire escape. At the conclusion of one complete trip with the flashlight he spied just the thing. It was a long, wooden-handled rake.

No—couldn't be, Murray told himself, inching toward it. Must be his imagination. What in the world would anyone be doing with a rake in New York City?

But as he got closer it looked more and more like a rake, and taking it in his hands, he realized it was no mirage either. With his right hand holding both the flashlight and the middle of the rake handle and his left hand steering the handle's end, he swung the rake over his shoulder and poked at the lower edge of the fire escape. While he did this, he took time out every so often to glance around and make sure he wasn't being observed. But there was silence from the alley, and the nearest lighted window was several buildings away.

Finally, he managed to engage the retractable ladder with the prongs of the rake and, using his entire weight, pulled the bottom end of the ladder to a position where he could reach it with his arms. There had been constant creaking during this operation, and there was still more creaking, then at last a clank, as the ladder came down the rest of the way.

Having achieved this much, he took a few seconds' rest. Then he bounced up and down on the bottom step of the ladder two or three times, testing his weight. Conditions seemed perfect. He started up the ladder and kept going after he reached the second floor. He decided to try the third floor first—for no particular reason, except perhaps that it was one more stage removed from Judy Wollman's apartment on the first floor.

On the third-story landing he shone his flashlight at the window in front of him and saw at once that he'd been right and Sandy had been wrong. The shades came all the way down to the bottom of the window frame. There was no possibility of seeing anything inside. He swore quietly and then, out of a sense of desperation more than anything else, brought both hands to the upper edge of the bottom sash and pushed upward.

And the sash moved!

No—impossible. What kind of idiot would leave a window unlocked after moving out?

Yet, when he tried again he was able to move the sash still further. Now there was enough of a crack at the bottom of the window frame for him to be able to insert his fingers. He could feel the grime already caked up on them, but what was a little more? He put both hands under the sash and pushed. By fits and starts the window rose to make an opening large enough for him to be able to climb through.

With extreme caution he eased himself through the window. Once inside he circled slowly with the flashlight. He was in a large room, most likely the living room, and it was practically bare. The air was saturated with the musty smell of an enclosed space that has been sealed up for a long period. On the floor was an assortment of the typical leavings of a tenant on his way to new quarters. There were some crumpled newspapers, a light bulb, a grocery carton that had apparently not been needed for packing, paper clips, nails, two or three pieces of silverware, a number of pencils, and a bookend.

Throwing the spot of the flashlight onto the floor in front of his feet, he edged forward. His eyes were gradually accustoming themselves to the darkness, and he was beginning to be able to distinguish objects on the floor as dim blotches without the aid of the light.

A little to his left he noticed an interesting patch of white and brought the flashlight spot to bear on it. On the floor it looked like an economy-size tube of toothpaste. He bent down to pick it up, but as he did so he thought he heard a noise from another room of the apartment. He paused. Nothing. Silence. Attributing the sound to faulty plumbing, he trained the flashlight spot on the tube and read the words ZINC WHITE.

So? He already had the easel; this was nothing new.

He brought the flashlight beam back to the floor and continued his search. There was another noise.

He listened.

Silence.

He kept listening.

Still silence.

The plumbing again, or maybe the wind. He wasn't going to worry about it; over in a corner he'd noticed a larger white patch on the floor. Approaching stealthily, he shone the flashlight on it. It was not a page of newspaper; it was a large white sheet, partially crumpled, with a kind of design on it. Probably unimportant, he told himself. Nevertheless, an instinct somewhere in his head urged him to pick it up. He stooped down and did so. His first observation was that it was burned around the edges. Then he smoothed it out, looked again, and gasped loudly.

The paper contained a charcoal sketch. It was of a pastoral scene—a mountain in the background and a bridge in the foreground. And the style was one he recognized instantly—Cézanne.

"Jesus Christ," he said softly.

His mind began to work. Miscellaneous facts fell into place —the two shootings, the robbery at Fischer's, the roll of color film Mrs. Aldeburg had found. Everything was—

"Yowp!"

Something had abruptly clamped itself around his right wrist. His right hand let go of the flashlight. "Hey—" He struggled to get free, but the grip had the tenacity of a bear trap. "What the hell is this?"

There was no reply, but the grip tightened, and he felt his right arm being wrenched up behind his back. Then in the small of his back, right underneath where the arm was being held, he felt something cold and hard. "Hey, who are—"

There was a sharp jerk on his arm—and considerable pain.

"What are you—"

Another jerk.

"What's going on—"

One more jerk. The pain was getting to be unbearable.

He got the idea. Whoever was holding onto his wrist wasn't especially anxious to hear the sound of his voice.

Murray became conscious of a slightly acid smell and felt a tickling at the back of his neck. The man was practically on top of him. And now that he thought about it, that thing stuck in his back probably wasn't a tube of paint. But why wouldn't the bastard say something? All right, Murray decided, we'll play it your way. He stopped trying to move his wrist and stood still.

The man holding his wrist sighed faintly. Then he pushed Murray's wrist against his back.

"What the—"

He pushed again, more forcibly this time, and Murray was jolted forward, his feet stumbling across the floor. There was another push. The man was taking him into another room of the apartment. Another series of pushes took him through what was apparently a doorway. On the way his senses tried to give him additional information, but it was having trouble getting through—the smell of a cheap hair cream, several grunts of effort with each shove. Everything possible to make the situation more unpleasant.

A final titanic push sent Murray cascading across the floor against a wall, where he lost his balance and fell down. The area where he'd fallen was soft, and he guessed it was a mattress. He was breathing quickly and felt pain in several parts of his body. When he looked up he saw dimly the man who held his wrist. The man's figure was barely distinguishable in the doorway through which Murray had just been propelled. The doorway was a faint rectangle of light and the man, a tall, broad-shouldered individual, stood in its center. He was nearly stationary.

Then he spoke the first and last words Murray was to hear from him that evening. "And you damn well better stay there," he said, and slammed the door savagely.

There was again dead silence.

Slowly, Murray began to retrieve his faculties. What the hell had happened, he wondered. Was the guy going to call the police? It certainly didn't seem likely. Then was he going to be kept in this room until he starved to death or decided to jump out of a window? That was certainly a possibility, he thought, judging by what he now knew and what the man who had captured him must know he knew. Oh, Mrs. Murray's idiot son, how did you ever get yourself into this!

He began to calm down. And a new thought occurred to him: he'd had a recognition. Something had registered in his mind a short while before, but he couldn't think what it was. Something . . . something . . .

The voice. He'd recognized the man's voice. Where had he heard it before? How could he *possibly* have heard it before? At the Museum? Maybe. At any event, he felt it was somehow connected with his job.

But this was no time for idle speculation. He laboriously raised himself from the mattress—whose dust was beginning to trouble his nose—and started toward the window of the room. On the way he massaged his right wrist with his other hand. The window in this room didn't look out over the fire escape, Murray quickly saw, but the scaffolding ended a few feet to the left of its bottom edge.

He tried to raise the window, but it wouldn't budge. He tried again. Same story. It seemed very much as if he'd have to smash the glass and climb through a ring of pointed shards, the way they did in 1930's Westerns. Then he noticed something between the window sashes—a lock. He chuckled slightly to himself. The lock could be worked from the inside and he quickly undid it. He pulled up on the indentations in the bottom of the lower sash, and the window came up without a hitch.

He stuck his head through the opening. If he sat on the windowsill, he judged, and extended his left leg, he might just be able to reach the railing of the fire escape. But it would be close. And if he could reach it, how would he get himself over onto the scaffolding?

He hauled himself onto the windowsill, feeling a momentary pang as he unwittingly looked down. His left leg fell about a foot above, and about three inches to the left of, the fire escape railing. He shook his head and climbed back into the room. He went to the door, tried the handle, and got the expected result. He returned to the mattress, sat down, and sneezed. He punched his left palm with his right fist. He sneezed again.

Oh, Murray, Murray . . .

Finally, he went back to the window. Once more he climbed onto the sill and dangled his legs. Oddly enough, there was still the same twelve inches between the sole of his shoe and the railing. He forced himself to look down, with the explanation that he was a masochist at heart. The concrete pavement below seemed to stare up at him from beneath the visor of the wooden fence at the back.

Which was better: to be shot by someone he couldn't see or to break a few ribs in a three-story fall? But who said it would just be a few ribs?

He began to envy those who had been brought up in religious homes. In the Murray household Passover received equal billing with Flag Day. Anyhow, it was unlikely there was a prayer to suit the situation in the Bible—Old or New Testament.

If the decision was going to be made it was going to have to be made quickly.

He took a deep breath and pushed off from the sill with both hands. For an unbearable fraction of a second he was in mid-air. Then the iron grating of the fire escape landing slammed against his feet. He lay in a heap for a full two minutes before his breathing slowed down and he could summon up the energy to get up.

All the way back to the West Fourth Street station his head bobbed from side to side as though he was at a tennis match. Every fuzzy derelict lying on the sidewalk and fluorescent homosexual strolling along the avenue seemed to be taking note of his movements. And the worst of it was, he wouldn't know the man who had held his wrist if he was three feet away.

On the IND he was sure the man across the aisle from him was the one. The man was wearing a very suspicious-looking felt hat whose brim just hid his eyebrows. He was reading a copy of the *Daily News*, but once in a while he would peer out over the top of the page directly at Murray. His head never moved, only his eyes. Murray stayed in his seat until the last minute as the train pulled into his stop. Then he made a dash for the door. The man glanced up briefly, shrugged, and reburied himself in the newspaper.

He hardly slept that night. Toward morning he had a dream. He was a white rat—perhaps a gerbil—and he was in a small wire cage. His keeper was a tall man—so tall that Murray the white rat had trouble seeing his face. The keeper had, in addition to height, one other striking feature: a grotesquely long index finger, which he continually poked through the bars of the cage. Whenever he did this, Murray climbed onto his treadmill and started off. Little by little, the index finger approached the rim of the treadmill, preparing to slow it down but never actually doing so. Instead, it would toy with Murray, making him run faster and faster. As he was about to collapse from fatigue he suddenly changed back into a human being who had to get up and face the day.

He dragged himself from between the sheets and sat on the edge of the couch. The traveling alarm clock on the coffee table said seven-thirty. "Ira," he called.

Some time later his brother padded into the living room in his bedroom slippers. "What?" His eyes were only half open.

"What's today?"

"You have to rob me of fifteen minutes' sleep to ask what day it is?"

"I want to know. It's important."

"Tuesday."

"Then I go to work today," Roger said, with almost vicious satisfaction.

"Sure you do. So do I. You have to sound so happy about it?" Ira turned and started back for the bedroom.

Roger leaped up from the couch and feverishly began to put on his clothes.

NINE

HE WAS THE FIRST ONE IN THE OFFICE that morning. Waiting for everyone else to arrive, he paced the floor. He couldn't read or do any work. He was wondering how to break the news, whom to tell. Acknowledging the chain of command, he decided Mr. Emerson would be best. Would he believe him? It was unlikely, but he had to start there. He would tell Sandy, of course, but later.

Sandy and Doris barged in at nine-ten. Sandy hung up her coat, whirled around, and said to Murray, "Notice anything?"

He inspected her unenthusiastically. "You've cut your hair."

She threw back her head. "Honestly, Roger, I don't know about you. I had my hair cut ages ago. The dress, stupid, the dress."

"It's very nice."

"Oh, Christ." She looked over her shoulder. "Don't you just love the way they appreciate us around here, Doris?"

Doris grunted.

"I made it," Sandy said significantly.

"Made what?" Murray asked.

"Oh-h-h. The dress, the *dress*."

"It's very pretty."

Sandy made a show of giving up on him and went over to her desk, where she took the cover off her typewriter.

At ten o'clock Mr. Emerson stumbled in, and Roger's heart leapt. Fidgeting, he waited while his superior meticulously hung up his coat, trudged into his office, and swung the taped briefcase up onto his desk.

While Emerson was conducting his daily perusal of the bookshelves, which Murray was beginning to suspect of being merely a delaying tactic, he organized his thoughts. "Mr. Emerson," he began, "I have something I'd like to discuss with you."

"Can't it wait? I've got to get out the final plans for exhibition procedures on the Cézanne."

"It's about the Cézanne, what I want to discuss."

Emerson had been delving into his briefcase, fishing out papers. He stopped delving, looked up, and said, "I suppose you're going to tell me the painting's a forgery."

Murray stared blankly at him. "How . . . how did you know?"

Emerson chucked the papers back into the briefcase in exasperation. "Look, Murray, I'm afraid I don't have time for jokes this morning. Some other morning, maybe, but not this morning."

"This is no joke," Murray said ardently.

Emerson sighed. "All right. I suppose ten minutes' wasted time won't kill me. And I can see you're not going to get any work done until you tell me. So let's hear it."

Starting with the acquisition of the pawn ticket the night of the auction, Murray told his story. He related only the facts first, planning to leave his conclusions until the end. Emerson said nothing until he reached the point where the man had sprung out of the darkness and grabbed his wrist.

"You see," Murray said, "I think I recognized him from somewhere. But I don't know where. That's the annoying part. I think if I could place him I'd know who was behind this whole thing."

"Maybe he's the Director," Emerson said. "Now let me get this straight. You first of all broke into an apartment in Greenwich Village—which is a felony right there—then you were accosted by some broad-chested fellow, presumably the owner of the apartment, and *then*, you say, this man locked you in a room but never once mentioned calling the police."

"And I think I knew him from his voice."

"And you think you knew him from his voice—marvelous. Murray, before you, uh, stopped in at this apartment you didn't happen to pay a visit to a bar, did you?"

"Mr. Emerson, this really happened! Why would I go to all the trouble of making something like this up?"

"You've only been here a few weeks. I don't know you well enough yet to be able to answer that question. But"—he waved his hands in the air—"continue."

Murray resumed his story and told of his escape from the room.

Then Emerson interrupted again. "All right, all right. Let's assume, for the sake of argument, that this is all true. What do you suppose this alleged attacker was going to do with you once he returned?"

"I don't know. Kill me, probably."

"Right. Now I believe you said he stuck a gun into your back at one point, right?"

"Yes. At least it felt like a gun."

"Okay, he had a gun. If he planned on killing you, why do you think he didn't do it right then and there?"

"I don't know. Maybe he thought I had some information to give him. Maybe he had to check with someone higher up."

"An interesting possibility. Well, go on."

"That's all there is. I got on the subway and came back uptown. All along the way I kept checking to make sure no one was following me."

"And was anyone?"

"As far as I could tell, no."

Emerson shook his head sadly and started taking things out of his briefcase again. "So you think that because you found a sketch of the Cézanne we just bought our painting is a forgery."

"Yes."

"Would you mind telling me how you arrived at that little conclusion?"

"Don't you see what was going on down there in the apartment? It was an artist's studio; they had a study for the Cézanne. The people who owned the apartment were the same ones that broke into Fischer's gallery a few weeks ago. They dropped that pawn ticket. *But they didn't take anything of any value.*"

Emerson drummed his fingers on the desk. "Murray," he said, "must we play Oedipus and the Sphinx?"

"I'm trying to tell you," Murray said. "Don't you see what must have happened? The night Fischer's was broken into, these people exchanged their forged Cézanne for the real one. What other explanation could there be? They tried to make it look like a robbery, but why would they steal two inconsequential pictures when they could have taken one of the most valuable paintings in the world?"

Emerson considered for a moment. "So you think they produced a forged Cézanne in that apartment. It would have taken months."

"They had months. For all we know they'd been working on it for years."

Emerson was quieting down. "Let me ask you this: why didn't they just take the painting from Fischer's? They were perfectly capable of breaking in. Why go to all the work of making up a copy when they could just steal the original and beat it?"

Murray was silent for several seconds. Then he said, "I can think of one possibility. The day after Mr. Gould was killed, that detective—what was his name? Nazi-looking fellow—Sugrue interviewed me. I asked him about who buys stolen paintings and he told me there are these very rich collectors who want the pictures so badly, they're willing to pay someone to steal them and then stash them away and never let anyone see them except themselves. The way they catch these people is, once a valuable painting's been stolen they keep an eye on their houses to see what goes in. If no one *knew* the picture had been stolen they could get away with it."

Emerson nodded; it was hard to tell whether he was being ironic or not. "All right," he said, "let's leave out police procedure for a minute. How do you know the occupant of this apartment wasn't just some innocent art student learning his trade? Every artist starts out by copying the Old Masters."

"Ah." Murray began circling the room, gazing down at the floor and smiling.

Emerson said, "Will you kindly remove that smug look from your face and answer my question."

Murray rested an elbow on a filing cabinet. "Art students copy the Old Masters—I don't deny that. But not this particular Old Master, or at least not this particular work. The painting's been out of circulation since it was painted. How would anyone have *seen* it to copy it? Unless they went about seeing it by some illegal means."

"Mm-hm. But if no one saw it how did the forger get a look at it?"

"I said, unless they did it by some illegal means. Do you remember Miss Reynolds has been expecting a package for the last couple of weeks?"

"She's never let me forget it," Emerson said.

"Well, that package had in it some film found by Mrs. Aldeburg—or by Mrs. Aldeburg's gardener—the night after someone tried to break in to the Aldeburg estate. This was shortly after her husband died. The film was blank; it was probably an extra roll. Whoever tried to break in was taking pictures of the Cézanne with that film. It was color film—very good color film."

"Again, however," Emerson said, "they could have simply walked off with the painting."

"No, they couldn't have. The Aldeburgs have a very elaborate burglar alarm system. Besides that, there's the same argument about police methods as there was for the robbery at Fischer's."

"I see." Emerson continued his casual emptying of the briefcase. "Is that all?"

"No," Murray said, "the shootings!"

"They're tied in too."

"Of course they're tied in. After Mr. Ferris was shot at I spoke to Mrs. Mayer. She asked me a very interesting question: Why did they pick Mr. Gould and Mr. Ferris to shoot? Then, when I visited Mr. Ferris in the hospital, he asked me the same thing. But he also unwittingly told me the answer. They were the only two people who *saw* the painting before the robbery at Fischer's. They were the only two in a position to identify the Met's picture as a fake."

"You're forgetting Fischer himself. He'd seen it too."

Murray walked around for a couple of seconds. "But his eyesight isn't so good!" he said suddenly. "That would account for it. Did you ever notice those thick glasses he wears? He was relatively safe."

"And Mrs. Aldeburg."

"To quote Miss Janis, Mrs. Aldeburg 'wouldn't know a Cézanne from a Max Schwartz.'"

"A who?"

"Nothing. Anyway Mr. Gould and Mr. Ferris were the only two who could positively identify the painting as a forgery. They were the only two with professional eyes who'd seen the picture before the robbery. Before it was exchanged for the fake."

Emerson shook his head for a considerable time. While shaking it he said, "Amazing, absolutely amazing." Then his eyes went to Murray's. "So who do you think is behind all this?"

"I don't know that," Murray replied, in a tone that intimated it was only a matter of time.

"You haven't figured that one out yet."

"No. But there seem to be some indications that it could be someone at the Museum."

"Indications such as?"

"I don't know, just indications."

Emerson closed the briefcase and swung it down to the floor. "Very interesting," he said, "very interesting."

Murray took a deep breath and relaxed. He hadn't envisioned that telling Mr. Emerson would be this easy. "I thought I'd like to let you know about it first. Then you could decide what to do. Whether we should tell the police right away or—"

"I've decided what to do," Emerson said tranquilly.

"You have? What?"

"First of all, you're going to get the hell back to the work you're supposed to be doing for the Metropolitan Museum and you're going to forget these ridiculous fantasies of yours. Forged paintings! God help us!"

Murray's entire body froze, all except for his mouth, which dropped open with the absent slowness of a damped phonograph arm. "You mean you don't believe any of this?"

"Not a word." Emerson's face took on a benevolent smile. "Let's just pretend it never happened. You haven't told me a thing, okay? I'm willing to keep this little discussion our secret."

"But it's all fact," Murray protested feebly.

"Sure it is," Emerson said. "Now you'd like to keep on working here, isn't that true? And we'd like to keep you, too. But when we hired you we thought we were getting a serious and dedicated student of fine arts, not a third-rate detective. If we were wrong in that belief, then perhaps the Met isn't the place for you. At any rate, going around advertising your exploits in criminology will only get you chucked out on your ear, I guarantee you."

"Will you just take a look at the painting? Maybe you can see it's a forgery."

"Murray," Emerson said slowly, patiently, "I *have* looked at it. That's what makes me so sure your whole story's madness. Listen, get these dreams of glory out of your head and get down to work, okay? Now, not another word."

"I'll think it over," Murray said gloomily.

"Think it over while you write this up for me," Emerson suggested, handing him a well-corrected typed sheet.

For the rest of the morning Murray's efficiency level was at an all-time low. And whatever he touched seemed to catch the disease. Ball-point pens skidded over the page making only ruts in the paper, pedestals suddenly planted themselves in his path when he went on errands, files whose location he was sure of had apparently wandered off with paper clips, rubber bands, and erasers during the night. What was he going to do now? Was there any more likelihood another member of the department would believe such a fantastic tale?

Finally, at a few minutes before twelve, after having spilled a vase of carnations that sat on a table in the reception room, he said to Sandy, "I can't take this any longer. I'm giving up."

She raised her head from the typewriter keyboard and gave him a quizzical look. "Yes, I've noticed you've been running around in sort of a daze this morning. What seems to be your problem?"

"Nothing."

She shrugged with her mouth. "Doesn't sound very serious. I'd like to help you, but my lunch hour begins in exactly thirty seconds." She checked her watch. "Twenty . . . fifteen . . ."

"Say, where are you going for lunch?" Murray asked suddenly.

". . . Ten—what?"

"I said, where are you going for lunch. Why don't we go over to the London Pub?"

She stared at him, wide-eyed. "We? You and me?"

"That's what the second person plural usually means, isn't it?"

"Well, Mr. Murray, I'd be delighted."

The London Pub was slightly better lit by day than by night. But only slightly. When they were comfortably ensconced in a booth Roger decided he'd put the problem to her. But without—if possible—disclosing his entire theory.

"Suppose," he said, "just as a hypothetical case, someone had some information that might be very important to the

Museum. Information about possibly illegal activities. What do you think they should do about it?"

Sandy's face exploded. "Wow, what have you found out!"

Murray, retaining his composure, said, "I told you this was hypothetical."

"Hypothetical," she sneered. "Come on, Roger."

"It is," he insisted. "Now what would you do?"

"If you let me in on this juicy piece of news you've come across, instead of trying to convince me you're taking a survey on the morals of museum employees," she said with a trace of haughtiness, "maybe I could help you."

"I can't." But he was weakening.

"I promise I won't breathe a word. It sounds fascinating."

"Well . . ." He told her of his return to the Morton Street apartment. He'd intended to tell her eventually, anyway. Then he gave her the same conclusions he'd conveyed to Mr. Emerson.

At the end she was silent for a long interval.

"Don't tell me you don't believe me either," he said passionately.

"I haven't made up my mind yet."

"So help me, it's the truth. Why would I want to make up a thing like that?"

"I don't know, a craving for attention, a latent exhibitionism. My psychology teacher probably would have been able to come up with a thousand reasons."

"To hell with your psychology teacher."

She patted his hand, which was resting on the table next to the silverware. "Oh, come on, I believe you."

The waiter glided over and delivered their food—a club sandwich for Murray, a tuna-fish salad sandwich for Sandy.

"So what do you think I should do?" he asked her when the waiter was gone.

"You've only told Mr. Emerson so far, right?"

Murray nodded.

"Well, there are plenty of other people to try. I don't suppose Miss Reynolds would be a good idea, but what about Mrs. Mayer?"

"I can't picture her believing me either. She's so logical. If I told her, she'd probably have *me* thinking I made the whole thing up by the time she finished."

"You may have a point there." She bit into her sandwich.

"So who's left? Ferris? Is he back yet, by the way?"

"He was in this morning for the first time since his little episode. Still has quite a bandage on that shoulder. He sort of looks like a fullback who forgot to remove a shoulder pad before he changed back into his civvies. Say, the tuna fish isn't bad for tuna fish. How's yours?"

"Not bad for lettuce and tomato."

"I thought you were having a club sandwich. There's supposed to be turkey in there somewhere."

"Is there? I hadn't noticed."

She laughed. Murray decided she had a very pleasant laugh.

"So you think I should try Mr. Ferris," he said.

"I don't see who else there is," Sandy said, finishing off the first half of her sandwich. "You probably won't get any further than you did with Mr. Emerson, but it's worth a try. I mean, you can't just let these people get away with this, can you?"

Murray agreed, and after returning to the European paintings offices he made Mr. Ferris's office his first stop, not even bothering to check in first with Mr. Emerson. Ferris was contemplating the official photograph of the Cézanne, taken for the Museum's records, which was propped up on top of a bookcase. He seemed to be imagining what the painting would look like on view, perhaps surrounded by gold-braided festoons and flanked by armed guards. If so, however, it was quite a task for his imagination, since there was no gold braid in evidence and the photograph was an eight-by-ten black-and-white.

As Murray approached Ferris's desk the curator gave him a smile of approval, and for a second or two Murray was ready to abandon all his theories and buckle down to work—the way Ferris's smile was mistakenly congratulating him on having already done. He could always claim he'd just dropped in to inquire when the Cézanne was going on exhibit. But he gathered up his courage, together with a hearty lungful of the musty air of the office, and determined to go ahead.

"Yes, Murray?" Ferris said cheerfully.

"Mr. Ferris, I have something I'd like to tell you that may sound very farfetched."

"Go ahead, go ahead," Ferris prompted. "The more far-fetched, the better. That's what we have young minds around here for, you know—wild new ideas."

"Yes, well, this one's pretty wild all right," Murray said, and rushed into his story. He was becoming adept at telling it by now, and the words came out more easily than they had the two times before. At the close Ferris didn't move but merely sat with both elbows on the desk top, his fingers joined at the tips. Except for the ridiculous lump on his right shoulder caused by the bandage he was a perfectly symmetrical statue.

"Where did you say this building is?" he asked after a time.

"The one where the guy caught me? Morton Street."

"Have you spoken to the landlord? Maybe the upstairs tenant was a perfectly law-abiding individual. People are apt to become pretty unpleasant when they find you breaking into their apartments. Maybe this chap just wanted to throw a scare into you."

"I doubt it. For one thing, he didn't live there anymore, I think. At least that's what the girl downstairs said. And if you'd heard him you'd have realized he wasn't just giving out idle threats. He meant it."

"But you say he only said a few words to you."

"That was enough."

"And you think you recognized the voice."

"I'm sure of it."

Ferris considered for a time longer, meanwhile going through miniature gymnastics with his lips. Finally, he spoke again. "Let me say this: your theories are a bit farfetched, but I'm willing to assume you're telling the truth about the factual part. After all, why should you lie?"

Murray was about to bring up Sandy's former psychology teacher but thought better of it.

"And it seems to me," Ferris went on, "if there was even the remotest chance of any of your—shall we say—conjectures being true I'd be inclined to look into the matter. We can't lose much by taking a few precautions, running a few tests."

"Then you believe me," Murray said.

"Only your somewhat fantastic adventures of last night. And I have the feeling you even romanticized those." Ferris held up a hand to forestall Murray's protests. "But as for these theories of yours—I have to admit I think you've been going to the movies a little too often."

"Well, I guess that's an improvement over Mr. Emerson, at any rate. He thought I'd been drinking."

"Much too down-to-earth, that man," Ferris said. "Very little in the way of imagination."

"But you will look into it."

Ferris was immobile for a second or two, then he clapped both hands down on his desk blotter. "Tell you what. Why don't you meet me down in the registrar's storeroom in, say, an hour. I'll have had a chance by then to take a good look at the picture. I don't see what harm can be done by some close scrutiny, do you?"

Murray shook his head vigorously.

The registrar's storeroom is one of many behind-the-scenes rooms at the Metropolitan of whose existence most visitors are entirely unaware. It's a large, cavernous place that, at any given moment, contains a wide variety of objects—paintings, sculpture, tapestries, furniture, artifacts, armor. The room is the first stop for all new acquisitions on their way to the far reaches of the Museum.

When Murray got there an hour later—having complained to Mr. Emerson of sudden and violent stomach trouble—Mr. Ferris was standing on an island of cement floor amidst two small oil paintings, a bronze head, and a Greek amphora. One hand was on the other elbow, and the hand attached to that elbow was massaging his chin. His eyes were fastened as firmly on the original of the Cézanne, which was standing on a wooden riser against one wall, as they had been on the black-

and-white reproduction back in his office. The registrar, whose name was Gabriel, was puttering around among the objects at the rear of the room. He was a short man with red hair and a red mustache, and he had a very shiny face. His cheekbones, the tip of his nose, and the point of his chin looked as though they'd been polished by hand and with great diligence.

Murray closed the large wooden door—one of a pair of double doors—as quietly as he knew how and approached Mr. Ferris. "Have you—"

But Ferris gave a forbidding shake of his head and indicated the registrar. "Mr. Gabriel," he called, "would you be kind enough to dig up the card on this for me?" He pointed to the Cézanne.

"Dig up?" said Mr. Gabriel, who spoke with a regional twang that was difficult to place. "We're working on it right now, Mr. Ferris. I can have it back here in no time."

"There isn't any rush," Ferris said as the registrar was retreating to the door. His office was about ten yards down the corridor. When Gabriel was gone Ferris explained to Murray, "I'd rather not have any more people than absolutely necessary know about this just yet. No sense stirring up a storm if your theories should prove groundless." He added, "As I'm bound to admit I'm sure they will."

But, having gotten a foot in the door, Murray was undiscourageable. "Have you found anything?" he asked. "Does it look like the same painting as the one you saw at Fischer's?"

"Can't tell. I don't remember much about the picture. Only looked at it for about two minutes and not with an eye toward authenticity. These supposed forgers of yours would be making a big mistake if they thought I was someone who could positively identify the painting as a fake."

Murray went up to the picture and started going over it inch by inch with his eyes. After a minute or so Ferris joined him. The curator scanned the canvas several times, then said, "I don't see anything wrong. If it's a forgery it's certainly an expert job."

Murray made no reply but kept on examining the surface. After several minutes of silent exploration he said, "I can't understand it. There's got to be something. I'm sure I'm right. They must have made a mistake somewhere." He continued inspecting the canvas.

When several more minutes had gone by, Ferris straightened up and stepped back from the picture shaking his head. "Listen, Murray, I think you're wasting your—"

"Hold it a second," Murray interrupted. He was studying an area near the lower right-hand corner of the canvas where the stream in the picture flowed out of the frame. "Do you see this?"

Ferris stepped back up to the painting and let his gaze rest on the area. "The water? So what? It's water, and very nicely executed, I'd say. Cézanne certainly had a way of—"

"No, look at these marks. Do you see? Everywhere else the painting of the river has been done in short lateral strokes. Here the paint's been applied in a very free circular motion."

Ferris looked more closely. "What's so unusual about that? He probably did one layer one day and came back the next and did those whitecaps. Would have been strange if it had been any other way. You know how Cézanne worked: a little bit at a time—first a drawing of the scene on the canvas in some dark neutral tone, maybe raw umber or burnt siena, then layers built up on one another, sometimes very thin layers, until the picture was complete. That's why it's so hard to tell which of his paintings are actually finished. The portrait of Madame Cézanne in the Fine Arts, for example—"

"But look," Murray said insistently, "this kind of stroke with the white here is totally different from the brushwork of the water beneath. Cézanne would never have done that. Even when he did different layers at different times the brushstroke was consistent. In fact, this doesn't even look like his brush at all!"

"Whoa! I think you're getting a little carried away there. Let's just calm down and take things—"

But Murray wasn't listening. His eyes were crawling around on the canvas like insects. "I think," he said slowly, "if we really look we can find other things. Once you notice one fault, you begin to notice thousands, isn't that true?"

"I suppose," said Ferris uncertainly, "but it would take quite a bit more than a few inconsistencies of brushstroke to determine that this was a forgery."

Murray's eyes were still roaming the canvas. "Wait a minute. Yup, look at this." He'd stopped at another area of the canvas, this one near the center. "The same thing."

Ferris looked.

"You see?" Murray said. "You see that? The copier missed the whole idea over here. It's a very distended passage—long strokes, long-drawn-out forms in the trees there. But right on top of that these very short circular strokes."

Ferris nodded once to signify that he was keeping an open mind.

"You see what must have happened?" Murray went on. "The man who painted this was letting his own style show through. That's what you get in a copy, isn't it? That's the way they're usually discovered."

Ferris reexamined the area, his hand thoughtfully on his chin. "I will say it's possible," he admitted after a time. "Not very likely but possible. I'll tell you what I can do. I'll have the picture taken up to the lab. Let Warrenvale go over it with his rig, maybe run an X ray." Harper Warrenvale, a South Carolinian, was the conservator of the European paintings department, as Murray had learned from Mr. Emerson during his first indoctrination lecture. The department was one of the few in the Museum that had its own conservator. Other departments relied on the Museum conservation staff for any physical work their pieces required. "It might mean a small allocation of funds," Ferris went on "—and the treasurer's down on our necks already—but if there was any chance it *was* a forgery, it would be well worth it."

"Do you think—" Murray began enthusiastically, but Ferris cut him off with another head shake.

"Here's the card you wanted, Mr. Ferris." Mr. Gabriel had returned. His cheekbones, nose, and chin seemed even shinier than before, and his mustache appeared freshly waxed.

130

"Thank you," said Ferris, "but I'm afraid we won't be needing it anymore." He drew Murray toward the door with an arm on his shoulder, leaving the registrar looking after them with his eyebrows lowered and one hand hesitatingly floating in the air.

When Murray got back to his brother's that evening—in an advanced state of euphoria—he found Ira sitting on the living room couch drinking what looked to be a martini.

The grin on Roger's face, which had been there since he'd left the Museum, dissolved into a frown. "What is this, Ira?" he asked. "You, drinking?"

"I can't take a drink in my own house?" Ira said surlily.

"Ira!" Murray exclaimed. "What's gotten into you? It's me, your brother Roger, remember?"

Ira thought for a second, looked at Roger out of eyes that were beginning to freeze over, and said, "Yes, I remember. And while we're on the subject, why did you have to wake me up this morning at six-thirty?"

"It wasn't six—Ira, what is this? Why are you being like this? Did the Market go down or what?"

"It's nothing," Ira said, and took a healthy swig of his martini. After he swallowed it he looked at the glass for a few moments, then went over to the table where the liquor bottles were kept and poured himself another from a glass pitcher. The pitcher, Roger could see, still contained an ample supply of gin and vermouth, but it looked as though, a little earlier in the evening, it had contained a far more ample supply. Ira walked unsteadily back to the couch and took a seat again. "'S nothing," he repeated.

Roger stamped around the living room for a brief interval and came to a halt before his brother. Ira's feet were on the couch cushion with his forearms making a bridge across his knees and his head resting on the bridge. "For God's sake," Murray said, "will you please cut this out? Will you tell me what's happened? If it's the goddamn Market again I can't see why it's worth all this—" Murray stopped abruptly, frowned, and moved his eyes from side to side. He slowly started to say, "Where's—" but he was interrupted by the sound of a key turning in the lock of the front door.

Martha entered wearing a camel's-hair suit and sunglasses. (On no previous occasion could Roger ever recall seeing her in sunglasses—even during the day.) She strode magisterially across the living room, saying what sounded to Roger like, "Left my hair dryer, that's all, nothing to get excited about," and disappeared into the hallway that led to the bedroom. While she was crossing the living room Ira held his martini glass out at arm's length and followed her progress with it in mock salute. There was some shuffling around in the bedroom, then five seconds later Martha reappeared. She walked back across the living room with the same queenly gait she'd used coming in, but when she arrived again at the front door she stopped. It was hard to tell because of the sunglasses, but she seemed to be trying to pretend Ira wasn't in the room. "I'm sorry about this, Roger," she said, with slight emphasis on his name. And that was all she said before opening the door again and walking out through it.

"Sorry about *what!*" Murray shouted as the door slammed. He looked over at the couch. Ira was shaking his head with clockwork regularity as though he planned never to run down. Murray stamped over to the couch and confronted his brother. "Ira, look at me." Ira raised his head languidly. "Ira, I demand to know what this is all about."

"What's it all about?" Ira repeated fatuously. "What's it all about? I should have thought that was glaringly obvious." He actually said "shove" for "should have." "Martha's walked out."

"Walked out? What do you mean walked out?"

"Gone. Left. Going, gone."

"But *where?*"

"Oh, I don't know. Her mother's, probably."

Murray gathered up breath to say something and changed his mind. "Has she done this before?" he asked.

"Once. Only last time she left a note. Want to know what it said?"

"No."

"It said, 'Dear Ira, I'm leaving you. Don't be upset. You'll find someone else. Love, Martha.' And at the bottom she put, 'P.S. Please don't pay any more money to Saks. Their computer is fouled up and they keep sending me a bill for a dress I've already paid for.' What do you think of that? Not Elizabeth Browning Barrett, is it?"

"Barrett—Oh, for Christ's sake, will you put that drink down and wake up! Will you wake up! Martha's gone and what are you doing about it?"

"Doing?" Ira said. "Doing? First of all I think I'm going to have another martini."

He got up from the couch with great difficulty and started walking over to the drinks table, leaving Murray standing in the middle of the living room floor saying, "Ira, Ira, Ira . . ."

TEN

I'M NOT GOING TO WORRY ABOUT IT, Roger told himself while getting dressed the next morning. That's the way Ira wants to play it—fine. If he's just going to sit by and let his wife walk out on him that's his business. Why should I stick my nose in?

He kept giving himself this advice at moments during the morning when there was danger his mind might wander. Lunch hour—he ate alone at a delicatessen on Lexington—was a long stretch of this nature. But at about two-thirty something came up to distract him forcibly. Mr. Emerson had been out of the office, and Murray had been sitting at his desk sifting through letters from collectors requesting information from the Museum about their own treasures. Answering such letters formed a large part of department routine, although it was Murray's conviction the office staff had better ways to spend its time.

Emerson came through the door and said, "Murray, there's a meeting of the entire department right now in the lab. You're invited." He looked directly into Murray's eyes. "I hope this doesn't mean what I think it means," he said significantly.

The Metropolitan Museum has two laboratories for analysis and preservation of its art objects. One, on the third floor, is devoted entirely to paintings, and the other, in the basement, is devoted to everything else. A curtain of tight security surrounds both; no one except Museum personnel and outside investigators directly involved in the analysis of a particular object is ever allowed entry to either one. The lab on the third floor, the smaller of the two, is nevertheless a huge square affair with a skylight that covers the entire ceiling, affording the room better light than that received by any of the Museum's galleries. The room is largely empty of equipment. Along one wall is an array of analytical devices: a large vertical X-ray machine, a powerful compound microscope, a lab table complete with sink and gas outlets and filled with reagents of the sort found in an ordinary college chemistry lab. The stifling, powdery smell of chemicals is constantly in the air. Generally, there are a number of paintings up for analysis or conservation work standing against the walls.

"If the painting should be a fake," Murray said to Mr. Emerson on the way upstairs, "—I'm not saying it is, but if it should be—what would happen to it?"

"Murray," Emerson replied icily, "if that picture's a fake, I'm the Aga Khan." But after a few more steps he warmed a little. "Of course we'd take it right off exhibition," he said. "There seems to be a good deal of sentiment around here right now for leaving forgeries out with a little sign on them: 'This is a forgery. Better take a good long look.' But let me tell you, if, by some miracle, this Cézanne should turn out to be a fake, I personally will see to it that it gets into the darkest, most hard-to-get-at place our storeroom has to offer."

When the two of them arrived at the lab Ferris, Miss Reynolds, and Mrs. Mayer were already there. They were all standing in a group looking, with varying degrees of interest, at the Cézanne, which was lying flat on one of the tables.

Murray went up to Mr. Ferris immediately and asked, "Have they checked into those strange areas yet? The ones where the brushstroke seems inconsistent."

Instead of answering Ferris merely looked around at the others.

Murray tried Mrs. Mayer. "Well, have they?"

"Go over to the painting, Mr. Murray," she said cryptically. Murray looked puzzled but obeyed. "Now wet your finger on your tongue." He stared at her with even greater bewilderment but again did as she directed. "Now," she said, "run your finger—lightly—over the area of the canvas in question." This time, Murray unhesitatingly complied. "Look at your finger. What do you see?"

Murray looked. The tip of his index finger was white. When he looked at the canvas again he noticed that there was a faint streak across the area of the picture with the circular brushstrokes. "Some of the paint came off," he said. "What does that mean?"

Miss Reynolds took over. "I see you don't know very much about restoration," she said. "When a painting is restored the overwork is invariably done in a medium different from the original medium. That's so if a future owner of the picture should become dissatisfied with previous conservation work he can always have it removed very easily. A great deal of restoration is done with water-based paint and other pigments that are very easily removable."

"You mean, this part of the painting was restoration?"

"I'm afraid that's true," said Miss Reynolds.

"But . . ." Murray started to say. Then he trailed off. "Wait a minute. That doesn't prove anything, the restoration work. That doesn't prove it's the original."

Emerson spoke, with a degree of satisfaction, Murray noted. "It certainly makes it look more authentic. It would have been a pretty careful forger to go to the trouble of forging restoration work—especially on a Cézanne. Most Cézannes don't need any conservation work done on them."

Murray, on whom all eyes were trained, said, "Maybe this one didn't either."

"What?" said two or three of the group in unison.

"Of course! This would have been the crowning touch. The final detail that would convince everyone the painting was genuine. A restoration job. Only the original would have had conservation work done on it. But when was it done? Who had it done? Has anyone checked with Mrs. Aldeburg?" He scanned the faces of the staff, all of which held traces of embarrassment. "There must be some record of when the work was done. It couldn't have happened before Aldeburg got hold of the picture because it wouldn't have required any restoration before then."

Emerson slapped his forehead and then held out the hand to everyone else. "Oh, this whole thing is ridiculous," he said. "The painting's obviously genuine. What are we wasting our time for? We should be doing our work and instead we're standing here arguing about some wild theories."

"Wait a second," Murray said. "Let me say one more thing. Suppose we removed the conservation work—all of it—and found that the painting was perfect underneath. Wouldn't that prove something? Wouldn't that show there was something wrong?"

There was general hemming and hawing.

Murray addressed Mr. Ferris. "Couldn't we have the overpainting removed? Couldn't we just do that?"

Ferris shrugged and said, "I suppose so. What do you say, George? The restoration is pretty clumsy in any case. We'd have to take it off sooner or later and let our own people do the whole thing over."

"Do what you like," Emerson replied.

"Fine," Murray said. "Then is it all right if I check with Mrs. Aldeburg?"

"Now?" Ferris asked.

"Why not? We could get the whole thing done in a half hour, and if I'm wrong I promise to shut up and not say another word about forgeries ever again."

"It might be worth it," Emerson said.

Thalia Reynolds, the organizer, said, "All right, why don't we all come back in thirty minutes and get this thing settled once and for all. Mr. Warrenvale"—Harper Warrenvale, the conservator, had been standing off in a corner of the lab trying to look busy and pretending to overhear nothing—"will you take charge of the painting? We'd like every bit of restoration work on the canvas removed. Is that clear?"

The group disbanded and Murray went down to a pay phone to call Mrs. Aldeburg. Somehow he felt that was more appropriate than using the office extension to place the call. After obtaining the number from Westchester Directory Assistance he had the Museum operator dial it.

On the third ring the phone was picked up and a quavering male voice said, "Aldeburgs' residence."

"May I speak to Mrs. Aldeburg, please?" Murray asked in his most well-oiled tones.

"Whom shall I say is calling?"

(*Who*, you idiot. *Who* shall I say is calling.) "I'm sure she won't recognize the name, but it's Murray, Roger Murray. Tell her I'm from the Metropolitan Museum."

"One moment, please. I'll see if Mrs. Aldeburg is at home."

(See if she's at home?) "Thank you very much."

Through the wire Murray could make out sounds consecutively indicating the gentle putting down of the receiver on a table or some other hard surface, the servant's walking away from the phone, and a creaky discussion between two elderly people each of whom had difficulty making himself understood. Then another series of footsteps was heard, and a slight, breathy female voice said, "Yes?" with considerable trepidation, as though the person who owned the voice had just been informed a distant relative had died.

"Mrs. Aldeburg?"

"Yes?"

"Mrs. Aldeburg, this is Roger Murray at the Metropolitan Museum. We just bought a painting that used to belong to your, uh, family. The Cézanne? You've heard about it? Well, I was wondering if I could ask you a question about that picture."

"Yes?"

"We need to know if there was ever any conservation work done on the picture. I mean, did your husband, uh, your late husband ever have the painting restored for any reason? Because of damage or anything?"

"Damage?"

"Yes. You know, they might have painted over some spots that were chipped off or something like that. You see, it's rather important we find out about this—"

Mrs. Aldeburg said something Murray failed to catch.

"Excuse me?"

"I said, I really don't know."

"Oh." There was a space. "There's no way you could sort of . . . find out?"

"Just a minute, please." Sounds from the receiver were swallowed up, evidently by Mrs. Aldeburg's hand covering the mouthpiece. Ten seconds later she was back. "As I said, I can't help you, but there's someone here right now who might be able to. Mr. Fischer. The man who purchased the picture from me. I'll put him on."

Fischer? What in the world was he—

"Yes?" Fischer left no doubt about what he judged his time to be worth.

"Mr. Fischer, this is Roger Murray at the Metropolitan. You may not remember, but I was over at your gallery the day after the robbery you had there. Now what I'm calling about, we need some information here at the Museum. It's pretty important we find this out—"

"What is this information, Mr. Murray?"

"Well, we have to know if there was ever any restoration work done on the Cézanne. The one you sold us. Would you happen to know if Mr. Aldeburg ever had the picture repaired for any reason?"

"Repaired!" Fischer was seething. "Repaired!" He could barely summon up the wind to express his outrage. "I'll have you know that picture was perfect, absolutely perfect! Not a mark on it! I had it inspected the day it came in. My eyesight isn't so good or I would have done it myself. And besides that, I have an affidavit from the executor of the estate saying that the picture had no damage whatsoever. Had never been restored. Never!"

"I'm sorry," Murray said contritely, "I didn't mean—"

"I know perfectly well what you meant."

"No, I didn't. The picture's fine. We're tickled to death about it. I wasn't blaming you. It's just for our records, you see. We need the information for our records."

"Well, you can tell your records for me there's never been even the smallest amount of repairing on that picture. It's perfect. It's in perfect condition."

"Yes. Well, thank you very much. I'm sorry to bother you."

"Good-bye, Mr. Murray."

"'Bye." He hung up.

That conversation had proved exactly nothing, he thought. Of course neither Mrs. Aldeburg, nor Fischer, nor Mr. Aldeburg if he'd been alive could be expected to go around publicizing the fact that the picture had undergone repair work. But that affidavit might mean something. In any event, he had the answer he was hoping for.

When he got back to the lab the others were waiting for him.

"Well?" Emerson said as he walked in.

"Mrs. Aldeburg didn't know a thing, but Albert Fischer was there and—"

"Fischer?" Thalia Reynolds burst out. "That parasite, that . . . that vulture? What was he doing there?"

"I didn't ask. Trying to buy some more of the Aldeburg collection, I imagine."

"So that's it, is it," said Miss Reynolds. "Will everyone excuse me. I think I'd better go down and speak to Mrs. Aldeburg myself before that man does any more damage." And she bustled out the door.

Emerson followed her progress with sarcastic eyes. When her footsteps had died out he turned back to Murray and asked, "So what did Fischer have to say?"

"Well, he was pretty annoyed at even the suggestion there might have been any restoration," Murray said.

"Oh my God, of course he was annoyed," Emerson said, and addressed the others. "What do you expect him to do? Shout from the rooftops that the painting was damaged merchandise?"

There were a few murmurs. Then everyone looked up to

see Harper Warrenvale approaching from the far corner of the lab. "Did you find anything?" Murray asked him before he reached the group.

Warrenvale ignored Murray and went up to Mr. Ferris. "I did like you said," he announced. "I took off all the white stuff."

"And?" Ferris said.

"It didn't look like any repair work was really called for."

As if the curtain had just gone up for the performance of a play there was a sudden hush. The faces of the three curators expressed surprise in diverse ways: Mrs. Mayer's by a determined frown, Mr. Ferris's by a pursing of the lips, Mr. Emerson's by an exasperated closing of the eyes. Murray was too excited to speak. Finally, Mr. Emerson broke the silence. "So what?" he said, looking around at the others. "So what does that prove? Maybe Aldeburg *thought* the painting needed restoration, maybe he liked to touch up his paintings the way some people draw mustaches on posters, maybe Cézanne did it himself, maybe a thousand things."

"It's not conclusive," Mrs. Mayer admitted.

"Well, I think it's worth a little more investigation," Ferris said. "Harper, why don't you take a couple of X rays."

Warrenvale went back to his corner.

"Just what's the point of that?" Emerson said when he'd gone. "Will you tell me, Stanley? Haven't we had enough notoriety with forgeries at this Museum already. A false alarm at this point isn't going to do the Museum a hell of a lot of good."

Ferris looked at him sternly. "A false alarm? And suppose it's not a false alarm, George? What happens when someone else notices the painting's not genuine? After we've been exhibiting it for a few years as an original. Will you answer that?"

"But it *is* the original," Emerson replied. "I don't care if it has a tic-tac-toe game in lipstick across the front, anyone with half an eye can see it's a Cézanne. And we just can't afford any more publicity, is all I'm saying."

"I'll make sure it's kept quiet, George," Ferris said. "Don't worry, I'll take care of it."

While this exchange was going on Murray had wandered across the room to the lab table where the painting itself was lying flat. He'd been looking at it for some minutes when he raised his head and called out, "Mr. Ferris, I think I've noticed something else."

Ferris glanced around apologetically at the others and said, "Be right back." He walked over to where Murray was standing.

"Look at this," Murray said when he got there. He pointed to an area near the center of the canvas. "See? There's a cracking pattern."

"Well?"

"This kind of a pattern wouldn't develop in a painting this recent, would it?"

"I suppose there hasn't been time for a craquelure to develop, no. The paint isn't applied thickly enough, and the support isn't oak or anything, like in the Renaissance, that would shrink or warp. What's your point?"

"Well, as far as we know, the painting was never stored in an attic or anything like that. Why should there be cracking in the surface?"

"Where do you think it came from?"

"I think it was put there by the forgers for the same reason as the restoration work: to make the painting look more authentic. But they overdid it. They went too far, don't you see?"

Ferris scratched his head. "Possible, possible, but there's no definite proof. Why don't we wait? I think you may have something here, but let's look into it a little more."

The two of them rejoined the others and, under threats from Emerson of tongues being cut out if word of the investigation into the Cézanne leaked, the meeting was adjourned.

Martha didn't show up that evening, but Ira left the bottles alone. Instead of getting drunk, he sulked. The best policy under such conditions, Roger advised himself, was silence.

But shortly after they had eaten TV dinners separately—Ira even seemed to consider it an imposition that Roger's aluminum foil tray had to share the oven for several minutes with his own—Roger could no longer sit still. "Why don't you at least call her?" he said. "You know where she is."

"I can't."

"Why not?"

"I don't know. It's not in my nature."

"Then maybe you should put it into your nature," Roger suggested, and the rest of the evening passed with no further words being exchanged.

The following morning at the office a great many problems flocked together to prevent him from concentrating. Besides Ira there was Mr. Emerson. Whatever the outcome of the investigation of the Cézanne it had built a barrier between Murray and his superior that would be hard to dismantle. Emerson had apparently put him down as one of the opposition, and nothing would cause him to see the situation in any other light.

Only two noteworthy events occurred before twelve. The first one was Mr. Emerson's promotion. At about eleven the Director called to tell him he'd been made acting chairman of the department. This wasn't much of a victory for Emerson since the Director had given him to understand that the post was indeed temporary, and that a new permanent chairman would be appointed shortly, probably from outside the Museum ranks.

The second event was the lab report on the Cézanne. The X rays had been very inconclusive. The underlying brushstroke could have been Cézanne's, but there were some peculiarities about it that might mean the picture was a forgery. The consensus of the department was that the painting was either genuine or very expertly forged. A complete nondecision.

Both of these events worried Murray, if for different reasons. To escape he thought back on the other events he'd either witnessed or heard about in connection with the Cézanne, in order to try to come up with something really positive. But nothing seemed to do the trick. He'd recognized the man from the Morton Street place. But from where? Emerson had received some mysterious phone calls, according to Sandy. But what did they signify? Chandler had suggested someone might be trying to frame him for Oscar Gould's murder. But who? And why? All these questions needed explaining, but none of them looked as though it would contribute anything toward showing that the Cézanne was a fake.

At ten of twelve Sandy noticed Murray's preoccupied expression and suggested they eat lunch together. Murray, with no strong feeling one way or the other, accepted.

"You don't *have* to, you know," Sandy said in response to his listless okay.

"That's all right," he said. "I have to talk to someone."

"Thanks," Sandy said.

They went to the London Pub again, where Roger thought he noticed looks of recognition in the eyes of some of the waiters. They settled into a booth, and for the first few minutes neither of them spoke. Finally, Sandy said, "What's the matter, Rodge? Is it this painting? Doesn't anyone else believe you?"

"No," he said, slowly rotating his water glass.

"What more do they want? Your theory explains everything, doesn't it?"

"It only explains it theoretically. Everything's circumstantial. They want some solid evidence, something substantial."

"Like what?"

"How should I know like what? If I knew I'd get it for them."

Sandy straightened out her place mat. "I have an idea," she said slowly. "Why don't you go back to Morton Street?"

"What for?" he asked.

"I don't know. I just have this feeling you might be able to find something."

"You and your feelings." He didn't say this malevolently. In fact, a smile was threatening to burst forth on his face. "I

144

think you're just jealous because I went down there last time without you."

"Listen, I don't need people locking *me* in empty rooms, thank you. I'm perfectly happy I was safe and sound in my own little bed that night."

Pointedly avoiding her eyes, he said, "If I went back there, then, I guess you'd want to stay in bed again."

"Now hold on a minute," she said. "There's always the possibility of too much of a good thing. I do other things besides go to bed."

"Mm-hm." Unexpectedly, Murray found that all this talk about bed was exciting him. He shifted around uncomfortably on the cushion of the wooden seat. "Well, I don't have anything pressing to do tonight, do you?"

After work they went straight to her apartment, where she fixed him a tunafish casserole. He ate it all, but after dinner was over he told her he'd have to teach her how to make some of the dishes he was good at—coq au vin, sweet and sour pork, eggplant parmigiana. Living alone in Cambridge, he'd been compelled to learn a little about cooking, he explained, although he couldn't really say he enjoyed it. She wasn't offended and insisted that he come over that weekend and demonstrate his skills.

There was a full moon out, and the rear façade of the building on Morton Street was well illuminated. You could even see shadows beneath the window ledges. As the two of them approached the fire escape Murray noticed some shiny objects that sparkled on and off on the ground by their feet. "Better watch it, there's a lot of broken glass around here."

"I'm watching it," she said, and slid her hand into his. "Do you mind?" she asked. "I'm a little nervous."

Nervous? Murray thought. Her? But he wasn't going to raise any objections. Actually, it was quite a nice feeling. He intertwined his fingers with hers and pretended from then on to be completely oblivious of any physical contact between them.

They came to the fire escape, and Murray saw immediately

that the last stage was down. No one had put it back up since his last visit. Which seemed odd, but he said nothing to Sandy. "I better go first," he announced after a quick perusal of the lie of the land. Before starting up the stairs he added, "Though I really don't see what good this is going to do besides possibly getting us *both* locked up in a room."

"I don't think so. My intuition tells me there isn't anyone here tonight."

"Let's hope your intuition is having a good night."

Cautiously, he began the climb up. The fire escape still creaked, and he paused every few steps in an irrational attempt to make it stop. At last he reached the third floor. He took one look at the windows in front of him and shook his head. Down below, Sandy was gazing up expectantly. "Shades are down," he said in a loud whisper. "Can't see a thing."

"Are they down all the way?" she asked in the same kind of stifled shout. "Isn't there a crack at the bottom?"

He examined the windows again. By God, she was right. At the bottom of the middle pane—it was a three-part window—there was a slight aperture between the bottom of the shade and the window frame. He looked down at Sandy and gave her a signal with his hand to indicate she'd guessed correctly. Then he crouched down so that his eyes were on a line with the crack. It took him a short while to adjust his eyes so that they ignored the reflections in the glass and focused on what was inside.

He blinked several times.

What happened next must have appeared to Sandy on the ground as though it had been taken from an old silent movie. His head suddenly dove forward, banging his nose against the window. There were two or three more compulsive dives, as if he was trying to smash the glass with his face. Next, he straightened up—no private has ever snapped to attention more speedily—and glanced down at Sandy. But he quickly abandoned the attention stance and knelt down once more. Then he went back into the nose-against-the-glass routine. Thump, thump.

"What in the world's going on up there?" Sandy tried to keep her stage whisper down and still be heard. "You see something?"

He straightened up again. For two or three seconds it seemed as though he'd been paralyzed by a Buck Rogers ray gun. Then the spell lifted all at once, and he dashed toward the stairs. The action appeared considerably speeded up for the next few moments as he raced down them. His feet made a metallic drumroll on the scaffolding. When he reached the bottom he collapsed against the last stage of the metal staircase. His breath came in frenetic bursts, not to be entirely accounted for by the trip down, and he pointed up toward the window.

He made sporadic attempts at communication that sounded like, "Original . . . (pant) . . . genuine . . . (pant) . . . up there . . ." Wild pointing.

"What?" Sandy said. "I can't understand you. Try to calm down. Just wait for a minute and then tell me."

He waited until his breathing rate slowed to a reasonable amount above normal. Then he said excitedly, "The original of the Cézanne! It's up there!" He swallowed with difficulty.

"What!"

"It's up there, it's up there!"

"How do you know? Did you see it through the window?"

"Yes, it's there. It's just sitting against a wall. No frame, but the painting's there."

"You're sure it's the Cézanne?"

"I'm sure, I'm sure."

"And it's just sitting there? Isn't anybody guarding it or anything?"

This question brought the conversation back to ground level. "I didn't see anyone," Murray said thoughtfully, giving no outward sign of the sudden lurch of his stomach. "That would be very strange, them just leaving it like that."

"So what are we going to do?" Sandy said.

"We'll call the police. No, we'll call Mr. Emerson and have him call the police. No, we better not call him; he'd never believe a word of this. We'll call Mr. Ferris and have him call the police. No, wait—"

"You're not calming down."

Murray took several breaths. "Before we call anybody I think you should go up and take a look, too. Otherwise they're going to accuse me of having hallucinations. What do you think?"

"I'm game," Sandy said.

"Fine. Now let's get clear on just how we're going to do this. We'll both go up together—quietly. That's the important thing—no noise."

"Are you implying—"

"*Then* we both look inside. Once. That's all. Then we come right back down together—again quietly. And we go call Mr. Ferris. You got all that?"

"Yes, chief."

"And that's another thing—no sarcasm." Murray inhaled several more times. "All right now, I'll go first."

The fire escape creaked twice as much with two on it as it had with one, but when they reached the third-story landing the creaking stopped. They both knelt down, Sandy with a great deal more ceremony. "Well," she said when they were well in position, "that's the end of this pair of stockings."

"Shh," Murray said, after debating between a number of alternatives.

Both of them stared in through the crack. Inside, pale rectangular patches of light stuck to the floor, thrown in by smaller windows at either end of the room whose shades hadn't been drawn. Against the wall directly facing them sat the Cézanne. There could be no mistaking it; parts of some of the rectangular patches were beginning to creep up across it from the bottom, and the rest was lit by the dim phosphorescence the side windows imparted evenly about the room. It was almost an exact duplicate of the painting in the Museum, except without the frame.

"The frame," Murray whispered. "Of course."

"What?" Sandy said.

"The frame. Why didn't we check the frame?"

"What for?"

"Well, they must have exchanged the copy for this one, but they took this one out of the frame and replaced it with the other one. They didn't just drop everything off, frame and all, you see?"

"No. Hey!" Sandy was still gazing through the crack. She looked up at him abruptly and mouthed, "What's that?" pointing inside.

Murray lowered his head to the crack again. It was a short while before his mind could interpret what he saw. One of the rectangular patches of light seemed all at once to take wing and flutter up toward the ceiling. But, before it got above waist-level, it suddenly plopped back to its former position on the floor. Then another fluttered and plopped. Then a third. Finally, he caught on. The light had climbed up something—some*one*!—who was moving around inside the apartment.

"Your intuition was wrong. Let's get out of here," Murray whispered, and then, as Sandy leaped up from her kneeling position, he furiously patted the air to signify that quiet as well as haste was demanded. They edged over to the fire escape steps, occasioning a minimum of creaking. But as they both straightened up fully, the scaffolding sent up a raucous screech. For just an instant all motion came to a halt. Then there was another sound—a rattle—apparently from inside the apartment. Murray glanced back and saw that the middle window of the group of three was no longer the off-white color of the shade behind it. He leaped backward, grabbed Sandy's hand as though it was a branch sticking out of a cliff face and he'd lost his footing, and started forward, just as another noise came from behind them—a fierce scraping, the whistling scrape of a window sash being raised hurriedly.

"For God's sake, let's go!" he said, struggling against his vocal cords, and launched himself off the top step, not looking behind at either Sandy or the window. He rushed headlong down the steps tugging her hand, which put up intermittent resistance. Before the fifth step he heard the first soft, eerie thump of air overhead and almost instantaneously the tinkle of a pane of glass shattering. But the sound was far away, probably from the building in back of Morton Street. He catapulted down the remainder of the first iron flight, still with Sandy's hand in tow. As the two of them barreled around the stanchion into the second-floor landing there was another thump, this time followed immediately by a clang of metal that seemed to have come from the staircase they'd just abandoned. Impossible! Murray thought, flying around an upright onto the next flight—no one was on—

"What *is* that!" Sandy screamed.

"Don't worry about it, just let's *go!*" Murray said without looking back, and on the final word gave her hand a vicious pull. The momentum carried them both careening down to the second-story balcony. He raced onto the landing and set his eyes on the next and final staircase at the other end of the platform, but as he started violently toward it Sandy's hand, which he'd been holding as if it was the handle of a heavy suitcase, suddenly got stuck. Dead weight—nothing. He whirled around and saw that at the other end of her arm her body was crumpled into a heap on the grating. "What is it!" he said in a frenzy. "What happened?"

"My ankle, I think."

"You've got to try! You've got to get up!" He started pulling on her hand again. "That guy may be coming after us."

He dragged her to her feet and continued pulling. She limped erratically behind him until they were on the last staircase. Somehow they engineered their way down it, Sandy by dragging her feet across the steps from time to time instead of taking them one by one. Halfway down, there was another clang from a spot somewhere right above them. Sandy, in a voice that was plainly using every remaining ounce of her strength, started to say, "Do you think that guy's got a—"

But Murray didn't let her finish. "LET'S GO!" he shouted.

They were on the pavement of the alley, making for the street as fast as Sandy's ankle would allow. Murray looked over his shoulder and said, "Anyway, guns make a very loud—"

"Haven't you ever heard of a silencer!" she shouted desperately at him.

"Oh my God."

They came to the sidewalk of Morton Street, where they halted for a second while Murray swung his head to left and right; then he started pulling her toward Seventh Avenue. A phone was the main thing now, he decided, and Seventh Avenue was their best chance. He was hoping for a drugstore or possibly a Riker's, cognizant of what it was to find an operative phone booth out on the street in New York. Finally, they reached Seventh Avenue, which was relatively well lit and crowded. On the corner they stopped for a minute and tried to get their breath back. But after a very short time, both realized the effort was futile, and they silently agreed to continue.

Across the street was what looked like a jazz place. Murray pointed to it, tried unsuccessfully to say something, and moved off the sidewalk. Horns blared.

"You're going to get us killed!" Sandy screamed.

"Come on, come on."

The wooden doors of the jazz place came closer and closer, and finally they were through them.

Once inside, they collapsed against each other in the small dimly lit vestibule. Like two sections of an orchestra jarringly out of phase in a frantic modern piece, the rhythms of their breathing seemed to fight for supremacy. After about a minute of this, Murray regained some control and embarrassedly took his arms from around Sandy. "We've got to call . . . [puff] . . . Mr. Ferris," he said.

She inhaled deeply several more times. "We can't . . . go in yet," she said. She took a few more breaths. "Look at me, I'm shaking like a leaf."

Murray tried to put his hand on the doorknob of the door that led into the main area of the nightclub but found that he had difficulty directing the movements of the hand. "So am I," he said, taking in more air. "I can't . . . do anything."

They stood there looking at each other with weary smiles for another minute. By this time their breathing had slowed to a manageable rate, and Murray opened the door to the inside. Within seconds, a man in black tie floated over to them and asked if he could show them to a table. Murray said no, all they wanted was a telephone, and at this, the man, who had been scrutinizing Murray with much more enthusiasm than he had Sandy, put on a haughty expression and indicated the rear of the large room using only his eyebrows and practically nothing else. "Back of the bar," he said in a ridiculous Oxford accent. "And please make it snappy. The proprietor is very particular about—harumph—strays."

They threaded their way to the rear, sidling through openings where chairs were pushed in close to the tiny tables. The bar appeared endless, but finally they came to a rounded corner in the counter. On the wall adjacent to the corner was a pay phone surrounded only by a small rectangular lean-to.

Murray picked up the phone, but as he did so the band— two saxophones, cornet, bass, and piano—erupted. The noise level was staggering; it was felt primarily not in the ear but in the stomach. Murray got Mr. Ferris's number from Information with great difficulty and with a finger planted firmly in his other ear. Then he dialed it with the same hand that held the receiver, leaving the other index finger locked into the ear.

"Hello." Ferris sounded as though he might have been awakened by the ring of the phone.

"Hello."

"Hello."

"Mr. Ferris? This is—"

"Hello, who is this?"

"Mr. Ferris, this is Roger Murray. From the Museum."

"Murray. Say, I can barely hear you. What's going on? You having some sort of orgy over there?"

Murray explained where he was and how he'd gotten there, having to fight off Ferris's expressions of disbelief every once in a while, to say nothing of his struggle against the cornet and saxophones belting out passages in unison. But finally, Ferris understood. "And you think they shot at you?" he asked.

"I'm sure of it," Murray said. "Listen"—he didn't mean, to the cornet solo, but that was mostly what came through —"you've got to call the police."

"Why me? Why don't you call them yourself?"

"They'd never believe me," Murray said. "Please."

"All right. What did you say the address was again?"

Murray told him and hung up with a huge sigh. "Christ," he said to Sandy, "I feel like I just climbed Mount Everest."

"Would you like to come back to my apartment and have something?" she asked a little uneasily. "Coffee? Hot chocolate?"

"Hot chocolate? What do you think this was—a skating party?" But when he saw the look on her face he softened. "Okay. Coffee, maybe."

When they got back to her apartment everything was dark. Sandy went straight to the door of her roommate's bedroom, after turning on a lamp in the living room, and peeked in. She came back with a finger across her mouth and seated him on the sofa. "You stay right there," she said. "I'll bring you something." And she was gone down the long hallway of the railroad apartment.

Ten minutes later she came back into the room carrying two cups. "You probably won't like it," she said. "It's mulled wine."

"It's delicious," he said after taking a sip.

"I find it very relaxing. *Ow!*"

"What's the matter? Yours too hot?"

"My ankle," she said. "Ooo . . ."

"Hey, I forgot. How is it? Here, let me take a look." He put his cup down on the coffee table and got down on his knees. "Listen, I know how those things are. I had one once from playing tennis. Played two sets after the ankle went out, but that night I couldn't walk. And it was swollen up like a balloon."

"You're a great comfort," she said, and when he looked up into her face, he saw her smiling down at him.

He got back up on the couch and put his arms around her

153

and kissed her. It was the most natural thing in the world. He kissed her again.

She began to take her business more seriously.

But sometime later she said, "We can't stay here. My roommate."

"Oh." Well, this was the way it always was. Why had he expected it to be different with her? "Yes," he said, "I suppose I better be going. Still one more workday this week."

He started to get up, but she pressed down on his shoulders with her arms, which were still around his neck. "Oh, I didn't mean that, you don't have to go yet if you don't want to."

"I don't?"

"I have my own room."

"You do?"

"Turn out that light," she whispered, "and follow me."

ELEVEN

THE FOLLOWING DAY, which was a Friday, started out beautifully for Murray. The first thing he saw upon waking up was
Sandy's face, eyes closed, on the pillow next to his own. He
kissed her, but she only mumbled something in her sleep.
Then he reached over and took hold of the bare shoulder
that was outside the covers. (It was warm.) "Hey," he said,
"we better get up. Work."

She peered out at him through the bottom halves of
her eyes and gave him an expression of total submission.
"Hmmm?" she said.

"Work," he said. "We gotta work today."

She scowled, dove back into the pillow, and turned her face
to the other side.

"Say," he said, "I don't usually tell this to people, but you
really look very good asleep."

When she turned her head back around she was smiling
dreamily. All at once the smile vanished. She frowned and
said, "Implying—"

"Implying nothing. You always think everybody's implying

something. You say I correct people all the time; well, I think you're always worried about people implying things."

"That's called paranoid, in case you're interested," she said, but before she could say anything else he kissed her on the lips. "Mmm . . ." He kissed her again.

"Listen," he said, "we can't do this now. We have to get to work."

She made a noise of disappointment, leaped across his naked body under the covers, and slipped into a bathrobe that had been on a chair next to the bed.

"Hey!"

"So you think I'm paranoid, do you?" she said, and disappeared into the bathroom.

A really magnificent beginning.

But when he got to the office things started to change. He immediately remembered, and just as immediately determined to forget, Ira. Then he began to think over the previous night's events. And leaving aside his nearness to death, he was still disturbed. There were just these miscellaneous little facts that didn't fit in at all. The man he'd seen last night had to have been the same one who'd grabbed him by the wrist several nights before. And Murray now really thought he knew who the man was. But that was impossible. It was the one person in the world he couldn't be. Then there was the question of why the man hadn't pursued them more diligently. Sandy had tripped, and he'd had plenty of time to scamper through the window, come down the fire escape, and finish them off. Then why hadn't he? And, for that matter, as Emerson had wondered when Murray had told him about it, why hadn't the man finished him off when he'd caught him there several nights ago? And finally, there were all those unexplained oddities like Emerson's phone calls and Chandler's resignation.

A little before ten—he was early—Emerson entered noisily, as he customarily did, and said to Murray, who was sitting at his own desk and staring resolutely at the blank wall in front of him, "Well, the big hero. How's it feel to be a big hero? Not so good, I guess," he added, noticing Murray's preoccupied expression. "What's the matter? This should be the happiest day of your life. The happiest day of all our lives—we thought we had a genuine Cézanne, and it turns out it's a forgery. Why aren't we all jumping for joy?"

"Mr. Emerson, I'm sorry."

"Sorry? What's there to be sorry about? Here, take a look at this." He scaled the copy of the *New York Times* he'd been carrying over toward Murray's desk. It landed directly in front of him, upside-down. "Page one—no less."

Murray turned the paper right-side-up and found the article Mr. Emerson had in mind. It was on the front page tucked into the shoulder of a story about municipal corruption. The headline stretched across two columns:

MET AIDE UNCOVERS CÉZANNE FORGERY

Murray began reading:

A substantial case of forgery involving the priceless Cézanne painting, "Le Pont des Trois Sautets," recently purchased by the Metropolitan Museum, was exposed here last night when assistant curator Roger Murray of the European paintings department discovered the real painting in a loft on Morton Street. Mr. Murray telephoned Stanley R. Ferris, an associate curator, after Murray had been, according to Ferris, "shot at several times." Mr. Ferris then telephoned the police, who rushed to the scene.

When plainclothes detectives from the 83rd Precinct arrived at the apartment they found the painting and arrested a man tentatively identified as William Seddon, who was in the apartment and is believed to be an accomplice of the forgers.

Seddon, according to the police, has a record of petty larceny and car theft, and had recently been employed by a New York cleaning and maintenance concern, Barclay, Incorporated. Spokesmen for Barclay said they had no idea . . .

So he'd been right. That's who the man was. But it was impossible. He couldn't understand it.

"Well?" Emerson said.

"I just don't understand it," Murray said. "Something's wrong somewhere, but I don't know what it is."

"Oh come on, now, you've solved the case. Please. Please, let's think about something else." Emerson picked up the telephone extension on his desk and spoke into it. "Miss Janis, would you get me the conservation department . . . thank you . . . Hello, who is this? Warrenvale? . . . Yes, this Mr. Emerson. I'd like the forgery transferred immediately to Storeroom B . . . that's right . . . just leave it there. Make up a card on it and put in the furthest corner you can find. I never want to set eyes on that thing as long as I'm employed by this museum. Is that clear? . . . thank you." He hung up and looked back at Murray. "Well, that should do it," he said and clapped his hands together. "Now, Murray, I've got a whole new batch of letters from collectors here that need answering . . ."

For the rest of the morning, wherever Murray went he received congratulations. "You've saved the Museum considerable embarrassment," Ferris told him. "I apologize for my doubts the other day."

"If you think you had doubts," Murray said, "you should have heard Mr. Emerson. You were about the only one who gave me any encouragement at all."

When he ran into Elizabeth Mayer in one of the galleries later in the morning, she said, "I think you've done a splendid piece of detective work, Mr. Murray. Let's hope you do as well in your artistic judgments for us."

Thalia Reynolds's good wishes were confined to a nod as she passed him in the reception room and the simple message: "You've saved us all a good deal of trouble, Mr. Murray."

But Sandy was ecstatic. "You're a celebrity!" she said. "Did you see the *Times*?"

"They got my position wrong," he said. "I'm a curatorial assistant not an assistant curator."

"Oh, won't you ever stop correcting?" She shook her head despairingly. "Well, I think it's wonderful. I just can't get over it. Maybe you'll be promoted."

"It's not exactly the kind of work one gets promoted for around here is it?"

"You are the most pessimistic person I've ever met," she said. "Where's the painting now, by the way? The original, I mean."

Murray pointed to her copy of the *Times*. "Read the continuation on page 37," he said.

She flipped through the paper and found the place. "'The painting is still in the apartment where it was discovered,'" she read, "'while police authorities await word from the Metropolitan on how it is to be transported back to the Museum. A police detail is keeping a twenty-four-hour watch inside the building, and roving units are patrolling the area watching for persons who might seek entry into the building.' Wow!"

"Wow, what?" This was said mechanically by Emerson, who had just opened the door connecting his office with the reception room. He spied Murray, who was resting one buttock on the edge of Sandy's desk, and said, "There you are. I've been looking for you. I'd like you to take this copy of last month's financial report"—he held it out—"to Miss Reynolds. It's really hers. I just borrowed it."

Well, Murray thought, taking the printed sheets stapled in the upper left-hand corner, an hour after my great victory and everything's back to normal. He walked to Miss Reynolds's office trying to convince himself to quit while he was ahead. There was no sense bothering himself over any details that might not add up, when to do so would only bring down the combined wrath of everyone in the department on his head. As far as detective work for the Metropolitan was concerned, he'd shot his wad.

Miss Reynolds's office was at the far end of the roughly L-shaped office complex. When he got to her door, which was painted green (in contrast to the other office doors, which were a dull gray), he knocked once. When there was no reply after half a minute he tried banging with more force. Finally, he opened the door and peeked in. The luxuriously padded leather swivel chair that Miss Reynolds reportedly had had custom made for herself by Hammacher Schlemmer—at her own expense, of course—was empty and was in a position that suggested a hurried departure from its confines. The papers and an open fountain pen on her desk indicated that the departure was probably recent.

Murray's eye fell on the papers. Idly, he picked them up and put them down. Naturally, the correct procedure in this situation was to leave the report on the desk, perhaps with a note clipped to it, and return to his own office. But a certain unreasonable curiosity was keeping him.

In the middle of toying with the papers he noticed that the top drawer of the desk was partially open. He shifted his attention to it. Inside was the normal pile of printed matter, letters, and manila folders, but on top of the pile was a very unusual-looking document. From what he could see, it looked like a plain piece of typing paper with small squares of printed writing pasted on. A scrapbook? Thalia Reynolds had her eccentricities, but she wasn't completely wacked out. So what else?

Going against his better judgment, he opened the drawer. His first plan was to leave the paper where it was and try to get what he could while pretending to be standing there casually waiting for her return. But this idea was quickly abandoned once he'd read the first five words of the pasted-on message: "To whom it may concern . . ." He snatched the sheet from the drawer and brought it close to his face. His mouth opened, his breathing slowed down, his eyes flicked back and forth.

To whom it may concern [he read]

I think you should know there is a man who has a private life he would not want to talk about. I mean a man named Alan Chandler. Why don't you ask Mr. Emerson about this. I am sorry I cannot identify myself. I am

A friend.

Murray's eyes stopped on the words "A friend," then they climbed back up to the salutation and went through the lines a second time. After this reading he swallowed and adjusted his vision so as to take in the entire page. The words had been cut out from the body of a newspaper—Murray thought he recognized the style as Times Roman—and fixed to the sheet in neat lines, the whole thing executed with a high degree of care and precision. He continued staring; his right arm, the arm holding the paper, seemed frozen into a permanent *v*.

"What have you got there?" Thalia Reynolds, arms crossed, was standing in the doorway of the office. She, too, had the appearance of a statue.

"Nothing." Murray whisked the sheet back into its place in the drawer.

"What do you mean, nothing?" Thalia Reynolds said, striding forward and coming over to the drawer. She picked the sheet off the pile and reminded herself of what it was. "So you've seen this," she said indignantly. "Well, you've seen it. Now I think you can go back about your business."

Murray was tongue-tied for two or three seconds. "Is this some sort of joke?" he asked finally.

"Joke? I should say not."

"Well, what is it then? What in God's name is it?"

"I should have thought that was plain. It's an anonymous letter."

"But what—How—" Murray stammered. "When did it come? Did this have something to do with Alan being . . ." He let the sentence go.

Miss Reynolds took some time to arrange her thoughts. "Mr. Murray, I understand you know Alan Chandler, is that correct?"

"Yes, I know him."

She paused for a brief time again. "Well, since you're a friend of his and since you've come upon this letter by accident"—the word held hints of danger—"I suppose you had better know the full story. I don't think it would be wise to let you run around forming *theories* about it." She put the letter back in the drawer and closed the drawer. "We received that about three months ago. Mr. Chandler had been employed here nearly a year by that time, and we all thought he was extremely competent. Myself included. Oh, I had my disagreements with him from time to time, but they were purely on an academic level. Then. Then this letter came. It was in a plain envelope addressed to the European paintings department. Somehow it found its way into my mailbox." She slyly inspected his face to see how he was taking all this. "Well, I must say we were flabbergasted."

"We?" Murray asked.

"I showed it to Mr. Gould, of course. He wasn't the chairman at that time, but I thought he'd have a good idea what should be done about it."

"Did you show it to Alan?"

"Then we went to Mr. Emerson," she continued smoothly, "and asked him just what was the meaning of that part that mentions his name. He was very upset about it. He didn't look upset, you understand, but I could tell he was. He suggested we should take the matter to the Director and ask him to fire Mr. Chandler. At first. Then he changed his mind. Anyway, I had the feeling he knew all about this for some time but didn't want to say anything."

"Knew about what?" Murray demanded.

"Well, about . . . about whatever it was Mr. Chandler was doing."

"With Mr. Emerson's wife, you mean?"

"You put it very bluntly, Mr. Murray. But yes, I suppose that was it."

Those mysterious phone calls Sandy said Emerson had received—things were becoming a little clearer. "Did you show the letter to Alan himself?" Murray repeated.

"We didn't feel that was called for."

"You mean you dismissed him without even giving him a single opportunity to defend himself?"

"Please don't adopt that tone of voice with me, Mr. Murray. And let me remind you we didn't dismiss him, as you put it; he resigned."

"After he wasn't promoted," Murray pointed out.

"That was the course we decided upon," Miss Reynolds said, flattening down the lapels of her suit. "The Director thought, and I agreed, that firing him would be a drastic step. Too drastic, and with too much publicity involved."

"You were worried about—"

"So we denied him a promotion that, in all fairness, I must tell you he was in line for. Our hope was, he'd realize someone had discovered his little games, and he'd stop. In fact, he resigned, which seems even more conclusive." She refolded her arms and cocked her head at him with finality.

Murray was again speechless for a time. "And it never occurred to anybody that this note might be the work of a nut? A professional anonymous note writer?" he asked when his voice came back.

"It occurred to us, but, as I said, Mr. Emerson's whole attitude gave it a great deal of credibility."

"A great deal of—Listen, I *know* Alan," Murray said with emotion. "He'd never even think of doing anything like this. He can barely talk to a strange girl without getting nervous. He's one of the shyest people I know."

"You'll have trouble convincing me of that," she said.

"I mean, with girls. I know he's very outspoken about questions of art. He's very confident about his knowledge in that area; but with girls it's different. You don't know him. If you did, you'd never for a moment suspect him of playing around with someone's wife."

Miss Reynolds winced perceptibly. Then she said, "I think I knew him well enough."

"You didn't even give him a chance," Murray reiterated.

"We did what we thought was right," Thalia Reynolds said blandly. "When he resigned the whole thing became a dead issue." She came over behind the desk and made a show of adjusting the chair in preparation to taking a seat. "By the way, have you come to my office for a reason, or are you just . . ."

"Mr. Emerson asked me to return this," Murray said with distaste, holding out the report.

"It would have been perfectly sufficient to leave it on my desk," she said. "Was there something else?"

Murray slapped it down on the desk top and was about to

give her an answer but decided he couldn't trust himself. He closed his mouth and, with steam almost visibly escaping from his ears, stormed out.

When he arrived back at his own office Emerson had already left for lunch. That was fine: proper fuming required solitude. That woman! How could she be so dense? How could they do that? They hadn't even given him a chance. What kind of people were these he was working for?

Gradually, he began to regain his self-control. Then he started asking more rational questions. *Had* the letter been merely the work of a nut? If not, what reason could anyone possibly have for playing such an underhanded trick? He hadn't known Gould, but would the man really have gone to such lengths to obtain the chairmanship if he was completely sane?

A cavalcade of thoughts passed through his mind, each one more fantastic than the previous one. Some of them were questions, some answers. Finally, at the tag end of the procession came the most farfetched idea of all. His theory about the Cézanne being a forgery was sanity itself beside it. He tried to forget it, but was unable to. He tried harder. The only thing he could find against it, though, was its very improbability. Everything else—the facts, mainly—was in its favor. No, it couldn't be. It was out of the realm of the possible.

But he'd gone this far . . .

Well, there was one thing he could do toward investigating it that was harmless enough. He could take another look at the painting upstairs—the forgery. (He hoped it still was upstairs.) Last night on the fire escape with Sandy he'd had an idea about the frame, an idea that, at the time, seemed as though it would merely provide confirmation in case the police had arrived at the apartment and not found the painting, and everyone at the Museum had rapidly started phoning the loony bin after he told his story. That hadn't happened, and he'd forgotten about the frame. Until now.

All right, it was worth a try.

He walked out of the office into the reception room with

such a brisk step that Sandy, who was squinting into a small compact mirror and primping some locks over her left ear, looked up and said, "Hey, where are you going in such a big hurry?"

He didn't answer but continued walking until he was through the door that connected the office complex with the galleries. Outside a few visitors were wandering around, and the smoking lounge that overlooks the main parking lot was filled. In one corner of the lounge was a uniformed attendant. Murray went over to him. He was the same attendant who had first showed Murray where the European paintings office was the day—it was nearly a month ago—he had started working at the Museum. "Well, scout," the guard said, "heard all about you. You must feel pretty good right now."

"Fine," Murray replied. "I wonder if I could ask you a favor." He explained, truthfully, that Mr. Emerson had ordered the Cézanne—the fake Cézanne—he must have heard about it—sent down to a storeroom in the basement. What he was wondering was, could he just take a look at it before they shipped it down there? "It's still up in the lab, I believe," he said. "You must have a key to up there, and I thought you might let me in."

"Sure," the guard said. "Nothing to it. Just about to go on my lunch hour. I could let you in, then go off."

Murray's face showed elation. "If it's not too much trouble," he said.

"No trouble 't all. Follow me."

The guard led him up to the lab on the third floor and opened the door with one of the keys on a round ring that seemed to hold about a thousand. "There you are. Now when you leave just close the door tight, you hear. It'll lock all by itself."

But Murray wasn't listening; he was treading quietly over to the picture, which was leaning against one wall. The guard smiled to himself, shook his head, and departed.

When Murray left the laboratory a half hour later (being careful to shut the door as the guard had requested) his palms were moist and he had a slight headache. Also, he thought he might be losing his mind. Had he been a drinking man he would have made tracks to the nearest bar, and the cheaper the whiskey the better. But, fortunately or unfortunately, he was so fundamentally a realist that whenever he drank his mind involuntarily fought the effects of the drink. As if it would drown if submerged beneath three fingers or more, it constantly treaded water and kept bobbing back above the surface of reality.

He'd already used up half his lunch hour, and so he hurried out of the Museum and walked and trotted over to Madison Avenue. He went to a delicatessen that, along with the London Pub, he was building up some familiarity with, but when he sat down at a table he found that all of a sudden he wasn't hungry. He positioned and repositioned the silverware, played with the paper napkin, and then slapped everything down on the table when he realized all at once what he was doing. When the waiter asked if he was ready to order he told him to come back.

He fidgeted for several more seconds after that before suddenly sitting up rigidly. He fished into the pocket of his pants that traditionally held his change and found thirty-seven cents. Not nearly enough. He got up and went over to the cashier, a tiger-blond woman whose features looked as though they'd been made of clay that someone had forgotten to fire and that, after long years, had begun to settle downward. Very shortly her nose would droop below her chin. When Murray handed her a dollar bill and said, "Could I have change, please?" she gave him a weary look intimating that she had been put on this earth to change dollar bills for people, but why did it have to be so obvious to everyone?

Murray fended off her reproachful stare and turned and headed for the rear of the restaurant, where he knew there was a public telephone. It was going to be a long involved business.

First he found the area code for New Hampshire in the front of a battered directory that swung out from its batlike state of rest. He dialed the area code plus five-five-five plus four more numbers which he knew very well didn't matter to the exchange in the slightest. After some problems with regional accents on both his own end and the operator's he got the number he wanted. Then he dialed that.

Two rings. Three. Four. What was this? The season couldn't be over already.

In the middle of the fifth ring the phone was picked up. A squeaky voice that he thought he recognized said, "Yes?"

"Is this Bertram's Guesthouse?" he asked, just to make sure.

"Yes . . ."

"Is Alan Chandler there, please? This is Roger Murray. Is this Aunt Mel? Listen, this is Alan's friend Roger, remember? I was up there a few weeks ago." This all came out at break-neck speed. Then he thought he'd better add, "I'm calling from New York." And he said again, "Is Alan there?"

"Alan?" The word had had to push its way through a mouthful of food. Now there was someone speaking in the background. "Who is it?" Murray thought he heard whispered. Then Chandler himself came on. "Hello," he said noncommittally.

"Alan! Alan, this is Roger."

Chandler let his guard down and chuckled faintly. "Hello, Rodge. Where are you?"

"I'm in New York. Listen, something very important has come up down here."

"Oh, I know. I read all about it in the papers this morning. Congratulations."

"Not that. Well, it's connected with that, but that's not exactly what I called about. Listen, Alan, you've got to come down here. To New York."

"Yuh, I was planning on making it in probably two, three weeks. I guess the police aren't—"

"I don't mean in two or three weeks," Murray said. "I mean now. As soon as you can. Today, if possible."

"What? What are you talking about, Rodge?"

"Look, I can't explain it over the phone. I know it sounds kind of crazy, but you've got to come down here. I need your opinion. It's terrifically important, and there's no one else I can go to."

"Why can't you tell me about it? Is someone else there with you?"

"Yes," he lied, and immediately cleared his throat. "Now, can you come? Listen, would I ask something like this if it wasn't extremely urgent? Would I?"

"Well, there *was* that time—"

"Never mind. This time it's urgent, take my word for it. Please, Alan."

"Rodge, I'm warning you, if this is another of your hare-brained tricks—"

"No tricks, so help me. You'll come?"

"I'm probably the world's biggest idiot, but—"

"God, that's great! Now, if you leave within the next hour you can probably get here some time between seven and eight. I'll meet you at the Museum."

"The Museum?"

"Right. You'll have to come through the back way, naturally. The guard should remember you; he'll let you in. I'll be in the European paintings office. Don't waste any time. Come straight here."

"Rodge, I hope to God you know what you're doing."

"Trust me. See you later."

"So long."

"'Bye." Murray's stomach swelled and collapsed with a prodigious sigh. Well, Alan thought he was being the world's biggest idiot. That might or might not be the case, but one thing Murray was sure of: he himself already had been.

TWELVE

"Working late again?" Sandy asked—and Roger thought he detected a note of sorrow in her voice—as she packed up her belongings and put on her coat. Everyone else in the department had already left. It was five after five.

"Yes," he said. He was sitting in Doris's chair and drumming the fingertips of one hand on his chin.

"I guess I'll see you . . . um, Monday, then."

"Oh, listen." He suddenly woke up. "Are you doing anything tomorrow? We could go to a movie or something."

She raised her eyebrows. "Tomorrow? What's tomorrow?"

"Saturday."

"Let's see, Saturday. Yes, I think that would be all right."

"Why don't we say around seven. We could go out for dinner too. Is that all right?"

"Roger Murray, you're the one person I know who can make an invitation to dinner sound like the death sentence."

He laughed. "See you tomorrow."

When she was gone he sat back in the chair for several minutes planning out a course of action for the evening. This was just like him, he realized—to overdramatize everything. And weren't things dramatic enough already?

At five-thirty he went back to his delicatessen, leaving the Museum by the employees entrance, and ordered a pastrami to go. He brought the sandwich back to the office and ate it, hardly conscious of taking a single bite. When dinner was over it was still only six-fifteen. He went into one of the other offices to make sure his watch hadn't stopped, but the clock there said the same thing. He tried out several methods of speeding up the hands: pacing, making an origami swan out of an old Museum map, straightening up some of the piles of papers on Mr. Emerson's desk. None of these was particularly effective, and since reading was out of the question, he simply sat behind his desk and determined to wait it out.

At quarter to seven he got an idea. Alan couldn't possibly get here for another fifteen minutes—more likely, it would be another hour—and he easily had time to go down to the storeroom himself and make a preliminary exploration of things. Early in the afternoon he'd seen several attendants carefully transporting the painting—draped in cloth like a Detroit prototype before unveiling day—down to the basement, so he was sure, at least, that it was there.

He wound through the galleries and down stairways, stepping over lengths of chain stretched across some of the accesses and ignoring NO ADMITTANCE signs hanging from the chains. On the first floor he found a Museum guard—the same one he'd talked to that afternoon, the same one who'd met him his first day; he was beginning to think there was only one for the whole place—and asked him to come with him and open the storeroom door. The guard agreed without question, and hummed quietly as they walked through the hallways.

"There y' are," he said after he'd used his key. "Now you let me know when you want to leave, hear? I got to come back and lock up." And he turned around and lumbered off.

Murray entered the storeroom, which was abysmally dark. The air inside was exactly the same as the air in the galleries, and great effort was expended to keep it that way. What little illumination was available in the room came from naked forty-watt bulbs attached to the low ceiling and operated by pullcords. Murray reached up and tugged a few of them as he went down the central aisle. The dim light gave the impression that the room was endlessly long but very narrow. On his left were the enormous wooden cabinets, probably dating from before the Depression, which house that part of the collection the Museum doesn't have room for in its galleries. Inside the cabinets pictures are suspended from metal panels that have a network of circular holes punched in them as if they had been designed with an eye toward minimum air resistance. The panels slide out to allow the Museum employees and scholars from the outside to inspect the paintings. Other visitors are not admitted. Each panel is numbered, and the numbers recorded on cards in a file at the front of the room.

Recalling the arrangement, Murray reversed direction and retraced his steps to the front. The card for the Cézanne was, of course, much newer than the others and looked it. It was a bright beige color, whereas the others were a moldy, washed-out grayish white. The card told him that the picture was in position number sixty-seven. In this case, the information was probably accurate, although very often, Murray knew, pictures got misplaced and had to be hunted up. No one worried very much about this laxity. The picture was in there somewhere, and a casual search would turn it up.

Murray pulled the light cord in front of the cabinet marked "60–85," and opened the doors. It took a healthy tug to slide out panel 67 the first few feet and several more to slide it out to its full extent. When it was finally all the way out he stood back and looked at the painting. He was seeing it differently now. Of course it was the same version he'd seen up in the lab this afternoon, the same one he'd seen at Fischer's gallery the night of the auction, the same one he'd just exposed as a forgery. Nevertheless, he kept on staring at it.

After viewing it from a distance he went up to it and took

a closer look. He examined the brushwork again, and the crack down the middle of the canvas, which he'd already reexamined very carefully that afternoon. It couldn't be, he told himself. Maybe he *was* losing his mind . . .

Then there was a noise.

It was a small click, the sound that might be made by shutting the case of a gold pocket watch. Afterward, there was complete silence once more. All of Murray's body stopped moving simultaneously, except for his eyes, which strained to reach past the limit of their sockets.

There were more clicks: a series of them, this time emanating definitely from the direction of the door to the storeroom. Murray's view of the door was cut off by the cabinets, and he quickly sidestepped so that he was in a direct line with it. Then he slid into an indentation in the wall and kept his eye on the door.

Slowly, someone opened it. Since there was more light from beyond the doorway than there was in front of it Murray couldn't make out anything of the figure right away, except that it was a man's. It remained in the rectangular opening for several seconds, its head moving in a little jerky rotation, before entering the storeroom

"Who's there?" said the man, cautiously moving forward on the cement floor.

The lights! Murray realized. What was he going to do now?

"Is anybody here?" the man said, louder this time. There could be no mistaking the voice. It was all as Murray had surmised.

"I know there's someone here," the man said. "Please come out. I know you're here. There's no reason to hide."

Murray felt himself shaking in the same way he involuntarily shook when someone was taking his picture and told him to keep absolutely still.

There was a scrape of shoes on the cement as the man moved forward. "Is there someone hiding in here?" he demanded, raising his voice. He was still advancing. Suddenly the scraping stopped, and after a moment or two he said,

"So it's the Cézanne, is it? I guess that means it's you, Murray. Come out, please. You're only wasting time."

Murray looked over his shoulder and saw the picture standing outside of its cabinet where he'd left it. He was now beginning to be conscious of sweat building up on his forehead. If he waited another five or so seconds without doing anything the man would be able, given his present rate of progress, to see into the indentation where he was hiding. Something had to be done. His glance fell on the floor, where several pieces of cement had chipped away from the surface in one spot and were lying next to a small crevice. He bent down carefully and picked up one of the pieces. Pausing for a brief time to estimate the distance, he brought his right arm back as far as the indentation's wall would allow and snapped his wrist in the direction of the light bulb nearest his position, in the hope that with the bulb out he would have some chance of making a dash for the door without being observed until it was too late. The chip hit with a reverberating crack against the wood of the storage cabinet door, missing the bulb by a good two feet. Murray's head quivered into a locked position on his neck.

"Are you in the cabinet, Murray?" the man said, with a touch of amusement.

So there was still a chance! He reached down and got another cement chip. He fired again. This time the shot was successful; the bulb exploded with an almost humorous *pop, tinkle.*

Total silence for a second after this. Then the man started advancing again, now apparently with more caution. "What are you doing, Murray? You can't put out every light bulb that's on no matter what you've got there. There are too many of them."

Could the man suspect him of having some kind of weapon? It sounded like it. And that indicated one thing: *he* probably had one. But he hadn't yet determined Murray's position with any accuracy, it seemed, and he was becoming wary.

The scraping continued. "You'll have to come out sooner or later. This room has no other entrance, you know."

Murray waited. There was no more time for potshots at light bulbs. He would have to take his chances with the present illumination.

The footsteps were closer, much closer, now. But they seemed to be veering off to the left side of the room. The man definitely had the idea Murray was hiding in a cabinet.

Absurdly, he remembered advice Ted Williams reputedly gave young hitters: wait until the last possible moment, then wait a little longer. It seemed pretty well suited to the occasion. The footsteps were only a few feet away. He still waited.

Finally, the man actually came into his line of vision. He was bent over slightly in the stance of a backcourt defenseman in basketball. He was approaching the open cabinet where the Cézanne had been stored. As he came up to it his head turned to look about him.

That was it. Murray broke for the door.

The man spun around and broke into a run also. The quick complicated clop of two pairs of running feet echoed through the room. Murray was using his full strength. Run, run, get out, got to—

He'd stumbled.

His feet moved frantically, propelling him nowhere. He was going to fall. No. He was almost up again. Then he felt something around his hips: the grip of a pair of arms. A tremendous weight suddenly bore down on his, thighs. He couldn't move. He pressed his feet against the floor, but he couldn't get any further. The arms were sinking down his body; now they were around his knees.

He thrashed fiercely with his legs, but the grip held on. His feet couldn't get any purchase on the floor. He was losing his balance. The man's arms were still sinking; they were on his calves. With one desperate burst of energy he kicked backward with his right foot. The kick must have landed on the man's collarbone. The grip of his arms loosened for just an instant, and Murray's legs suddenly came free.

After one false start he was moving again. Behind him he could hear the shuffling of the man scrambling to his feet.

Murray dashed toward the door and in another second he was through it. The man was up now and already in pursuit. The main thing was to stay out of a direct line with him, Murray reasoned breathlessly, in case he was carrying—

The steps! For God's sake, where were the steps!

He had to pause a moment to get his bearings in the dark hall. Then he started off down the corridor. The man was some distance behind, but the footsteps weren't slackening. In the darkness Murray careened wildly, trying to locate the stairway. There was practically no light at all. The rap of shoes on marble was coming closer. Where the hell was it?

He found it. He leaped up and took the stairs two at a time. The man was at the bottom in another second and starting up also. Four more steps. Only four.

Then it happened: he fell flat on his face. His legs slid down two or three steps. There was no possible way for him to get up.

For what seemed an endless time nothing happened. Then something whizzed by him—something that, as it flew past, resembled a mailbag being whisked from its hook by a passing train. There was an explosion that stabbed at the midsection. This dissolved into sounds of scuffling. Looking down along his body, he saw that the struggle was taking place at the bottom of the stairwell. It was too dark to make out who the participants were, but they were enmeshed together on the floor and bouncing around crazily.

Murray watched fixedly, as though enough concentration on his part might peel away the darkness.

But only his ears were of any use. There were groans of extreme discomfort. And more groans. Thumps: the noise of the flesh of a hard part of one body meeting the soft part of another. More thumps. Still more. Finally, a dull repeated rhythmic pounding emerged from the racket, and then silence.

One of the two figures disengaged himself from the pile and raised himself and started slowly, laboriously, up the steps. He was breathing in gasps that moved his whole body up and down, as though his lungs were a loosely mounted car engine and his body the body of the car. He was hunched over in exhaustion.

Murray stared at him, hypnotized, until he reached a point on the steps where the dim light from upstairs in the gallery fell on his face. At that moment all of Murray's emotions over the entire evening erupted in a single word.

"ALAN!"

Alan Chandler stopped halfway up the steps and stood above Murray's figure. He was still breathing too violently to speak.

"Alan! Alan, Alan, are you okay!"

His panting gave way briefly to ". . . Think so . . ."

Murray's eyes widened. "Did he—Did he have a gun?"

Chandler wiped some sweat off his forehead with a sleeve. His tweed sports jacket was covered with a smattering of pale gray dirt. ". . . Sounded like it . . ."

Both of them held their positions for a moment, Murray looking up at his friend's figure, which was still vibrating, though no longer with such force.

Finally, Murray said, "God, what happened!"

"What happened," Chandler panted, "was . . . I saw this guy pull out a gun. That's . . . what happened."

The opening of Murray's mouth preceded his words by a good interval. "And you just—"

Chandler nodded and swallowed simultaneously. "Threw myself at him. That's about the size of it." He was getting his breath back.

What did you say to someone in a case like this, Murray wondered. What could you possibly say? He tried to convey his thoughts with a weak smile. "How did you know—"

Chandler indicated the top of the stairway with his head. A man was standing there, a man wearing the uniform of a Museum guard. "He told me you were here," Chandler said. "I kind of got worried when he told me that. All kidding aside, Rodge, I know you're not the type to go around making phone calls just to scare people." He smiled. Then he appeared to remember something and his expression changed.

176

"Do you know him, Rodge?" He motioned in the direction of the man lying at the bottom of the stairs.

"I know him," Murray admitted.

"Kind of strange. He doesn't look like a thug. Dressed in a goddamn business suit. He could be a curator."

Murray nodded. "He is a curator."

"What! I was just kidding," Chandler said. He snorted. "You're pulling my leg, Rodge. If he's a curator, how come I don't recognize him?"

"He was your replacement. His name's Ferris."

THIRTEEN

IT WAS SIX O'CLOCK THE NEXT EVENING. As if there was an invisible network of pipelines from the drinks table to each glass, alcohol was mysteriously draining from the bottles and materializing in the glasses with apparently no help from Ira. All five of them had glasses: Martha and Sandy had highball glasses with gin-and-tonics, Roger a lowball glass with scotch and water, Alan Chandler a wineglass with dry vermouth on the rocks ("Oh, Alan," everyone had said), and Ira a martini glass with his usual martini (three jiggers of gin and a bow in the direction of Paris; he was no longer bothering with any amenities such as olives). Several items were in need of celebration: Martha's return, Roger's solving of the Cézanne case (as it was becoming known), apologies all around between Chandler and the Museum, and even, Roger insisted, his own resignation from the Metropolitan. All these events had occurred earlier in the day.

About Martha's return Ira was being very tight-lipped. The two of them had appeared around four o'clock that afternoon, Ira having been out of the apartment when Murray woke up at ten-thirty. Roger thought he knew what had happened, though: Ira had finally mustered his determination

178

(or kicked his inhibitions, might have been more accurate) and gone out to Brooklyn. There had been an argument, no doubt, on the doorstep of Martha's parents' semidetached house—Martha wasn't one for courtesy-no-matter-what—but she'd agreed finally at least to let him inside.

Once alone with her where they wouldn't be disturbed, Ira had turned on the boyish charm with which he was well provided. This was a commodity he kept vacuum-sealed (to retain freshness) until strategic moments, but when they came he could be pitifully endearing.

Now, as evidence of the new leaf that had been turned over, he would constantly ask Martha if there was anything he could get her or if everything was all right. For her part, Martha maintained an expression of cynical doubt, as if to ask rhetorically how long all this was going to go on. And, Roger thought, who could say.

"Now give me this again, Rodge," Alan Chandler suddenly said. Of the five his enunciation had suffered the least damage over the last half hour. "How did Ferris worm his way in in the first place?"

Roger took a sip of scotch, straightened out his neck to open up the channels, and said, "Well, the first thing he had to do was make sure there would be an opening. When the old chairman—the one before Gould—resigned, the plan was not to hire anybody new. Ferris had applied for a job before, and been turned down, but only because there was no room for him. You told me, Alan, the consensus was that the department was getting too big, and the Director was just going to promote someone to the chairmanship and let everything else stand. Ferris had to see to it that someone else left the department."

"Wait a minute," Chandler said. "You mean he planned all this that far back? How did he know the painting would come to the Met? How did he even know Aldeburg was going to die?"

"Aldeburg was sick. Not many people knew that, but Ferris did. He just had to assume the painting would find its way to the Met sooner or later. This wasn't a bad assumption. So what he did was, he arranged things so you'd either quit or get fired, it didn't matter which. He was counting on Emerson there. In fact, Emerson was the key to the whole plan. Ferris must have studied the personalities of the members of the department and found one whose quirks fitted into his plans beautifully. In more ways than one. First of all, Emerson had a wife who wasn't particularly loyal and who had a reputation for gallivanting. He bought her off."

There were some murmurs. "How do you know that?" Sandy asked.

"I'm guessing, but it seems likely. She sounds like something of a bitch. He paid her to make phone calls to Emerson from Connecticut, giving him the impression that someone—he didn't know who, of course, till later—was shacking up with her every weekend. Then he sent the anonymous letter. Emerson was supposed to put two and two together and realize who it was that was going off with his wife to Connecticut. He was also counting on Thalia Reynolds's puritanism there. Between the two of them, Ferris thought, they'd make sure Alan lost his job one way or another. That happened, but probably not the way Ferris had intended."

"Okay, so now he's in the Museum," Ira said furrily, "now what?"

"Then Aldeburg died and the painting was sold to Fischer's. Ferris must have known Mrs. Aldeburg well enough to be sure she'd sell the picture. He didn't know Fischer would buy it, but as it turned out, that was perfect for him. The painting was sitting in a place where people from the Museum would go over and look at it one by one, or at least a few at a time. Okay, then he staged this phony robbery; shot Gould, the only man who had seen the picture before the robbery (besides himself); had himself shot (at least one other person was involved)—for consistency, since he'd also seen the picture; and—"

"I get it," Ira said. "He staged this robbery, but he didn't rob anything. What he did was exchange the fake Cézanne for the real one. Then he had to shoot Gould because he was the only man who could identify the picture in Fischer's as the fake, since he'd seen it before the exchange."

Murray smiled mischievously. "No," he said, scanning the faces of the other four as he spoke, "he shot Gould because Gould was the only man in a position to identify the picture in Fischer's after the robbery as the *real* one."

"What!" was the general reaction.

"That's right. You see, everyone was supposed to think just what Ira said. Everything Ferris arranged was intended to convince people that an exchange had been made. A phony robbery where nothing of any value was taken, a man sneaking into the Aldeburg estate to photograph the picture so a copy could be made, the shooting of Gould and himself, supposedly the only two who could spot the forgery. And the greatest stroke of all: forcing a pawn ticket on me that would lead straight to the alleged forger's studio."

"You mean all that was intentional?" Sandy said, astonished.

"Mm-hm. The janitor at Fischer's was Ferris's one other confederate. The police already have him, of course. You see, he was the man who captured me that first night in the apartment."

"How could that be?" Sandy said.

"Exactly what I thought once I realized who he was. Why would the same man give me a pawn ticket and then go down there and make threats on my life. How could he even know where the place was? That was why I couldn't figure out who he was for so long; the janitor at Fischer's seemed to be the one person he couldn't possibly be. Unless. Unless the whole plan was to get me down there, and the janitor was in on it. Which was, of course, the only possible answer that made any sense."

"Now hold on here a second, hold on," Ira said, his glass waving unsteadily in the air, half a martini sloshing around inside. "You say the picture in Fischer's after the robbery was the real one. How do you explain that? They didn't make another exchange, did they?"

"They never made any exchange at all. Everything they did

had two reasons: what it was supposed to look like they were doing, and what they actually did. The robbery was supposed to look like they were making an exchange of the fake for the real picture. What they actually did was doctor the real picture to make it look like a fake. They put some clumsy restoration work in spots to make it seem as though the forgers had gone too far; they put some phony cracking on the canvas—again overenthusiasm, supposedly, by the forgers; they probably even did something to the surface that would show up suspiciously in X rays."

"How did you figure all this out?" Martha wanted to know.

"There were just too many little things that didn't fit in with the theory that the picture was a forgery. Things were too convenient. For example, the first night I went to the Morton Street place I found a rake lying on the ground. Can you imagine a rake in New York City? And then there was the question of why that guy didn't just shoot me then and there after he caught me. Or phone the police. Or anything. But two things tipped me off finally: first, I realized who that guy was, and second, I went up to the lab yesterday morning and looked at the frame of the painting in the Museum."

"What—oops." Ira had barely managed to save his martini from a messy splashdown on the rug. "What did the frame have to do with anything?"

"Well, don't you see? If there really had been an exchange there would have been scratches on the frame. They would have had to pry out the old nails and put them back again. You see, they didn't make a duplicate frame; I found that out when Sandy and I went down there together. The supposedly real picture had no frame. Anyway, yesterday when I checked there were no scratches. Those nails hadn't been removed for fifty years."

"What I want to know," said Sandy, who was beginning to get a dreamy look in her eyes, "is, what was the point of all this? Was it just some kind of high-class vandalism, or did Ferris really intend to get hold of the original somehow?"

"You're drunk," Roger pointed out. "Naturally, they intended to get the original. It was very clever. Here again they were counting on Emerson's personality very heavily. Once everybody thought the Museum version was the forgery Emerson would be up in arms wanting to get rid of it. The Museum couldn't let it go or destroy it, but Ferris must have been counting on just what did happen happening. That was, of course, Emerson ordering the picture down to an obscure place in the storeroom. What else could he do with it, assuming he was adamant against leaving it out on exhibition? And that was the only danger."

"So once it was down there in the storeroom," Chandler supplied, "where everything is out of order anyway, he could just walk off with it one night without anybody noticing."

"Exactly," Murray said. "I don't think he was going to take it last night, though. He probably just wanted to see where it was so he could plan out the logistics of a later burglary."

"All right," Ira said, "one more question and then I'm through. Why the hell did he go to all this trouble? He could have just exchanged a fake picture for the real one when it was at Fischer's. For that matter, he could have just walked off with the real one at that time without leaving a forgery behind."

"He couldn't just walk off with it," Roger said. "The policeman who questioned me after Gould was killed explained that. You see, the racket works this way: there are some very well-fixed collectors who are willing to go to a lot of expense to get paintings even if they have to get someone to steal them for them. They can't show the paintings, of course, but that's okay. All they're interested in is being able to look at the pictures in solitude and have the satisfaction of knowing that they own the original. But the way they catch these people is by watching their houses—the police pretty much know who they are—right after a valuable painting is stolen. The trick was to steal the Cézanne without anyone knowing it was stolen—not such an easy thing. Even if they'd merely exchanged the Cézanne for a copy at Fischer's someone might have caught on right away, and that would have been that. I wouldn't be surprised if this collector—whoever he is—put it in his contract with Ferris that he was to steal the painting without anyone realizing it had been stolen, otherwise there was no deal."

"That's fantastic," Martha contributed.

"Oh, I don't know," Ira said, breaking his promise of a few moments before. "If it had been me now, I'd have made an agreement with this rich collector and then slipped *him* the forgery. Would have saved a lot of trouble all around."

"I doubt whether that would have been possible," Roger said seriously. "This collector, I'd almost be certain, was one of the few people who had seen the real painting when Aldeburg still had it. I can't imagine he would have trusted Ferris with a scheme like this if he hadn't. This was the one way, you see, whereby the collector would know he had the original, the Museum would think *they* had the original (after they'd recovered the fake), and the police wouldn't be out investigating the robbery of a million-dollar Cézanne, which wouldn't have been so pleasant for this collector either. Everyone would be happy."

"Everyone except you, Rodge," Sandy reminded him. "You've resigned, I hear."

"Oh, well, I think that was the best thing for all concerned. I'm just not cut out for that sort of work."

"What are you going to do?" Ira asked. "Join the police force?"

"I haven't decided yet," Roger answered stubbornly. "Maybe I'll write a book about it."

"Oh, sure, sure," Ira said.

"Anyway," Roger said, looking over at Chandler, "I hear they've asked you to come back, Alan. So it won't be a total loss. Are you going to accept?"

"Probably. I like the Museum of Fine Arts, but I've probably lost my job there by now anyway, and I would like to be back in New York. Actually," he added, "they're considering me for chairman."

"Well," Roger said, "wouldn't that be ironic?"

"Yes," Sandy piped up, looking over at him, "wouldn't it?"

G 7 R 3 1 9 1. H.225